The Summer of Owen Todd

The Summer of Owen Todd

TONY ABBOTT

FARRAR STRAUS GIROUX
NEW YORK

Farrar Straus Giroux Books for Young Readers
An imprint of Macmillan Publishing Group, LLC
175 Fifth Avenue, New York 10010

Printed in the United States of America by LSC Communications,
Harrisonburg, Virginia
Designed by Andrew Arnold
First edition, 2017
1   3   5   7   9   10   8   6   4   2

mackids.com

Library of Congress Cataloging-in-Publication Data

Names: Abbott, Tony, 1952– author.
Title: The summer of Owen Todd / Tony Abbott.
Description: First edition. | New York : Farrar Straus Giroux, 2017. |
    Summary: In the touristy town of Cape Cod, eleven-year-old Owen faces
    a dilemma when his best friend Sean is sexually abused by a trusted adult,
    but warns Owen not tell anyone what is happening. |
Identifiers: LCCN 2016058780 (print) | LCCN 2017025282 (ebook) |
    ISBN 9780374305529 (ebook) | ISBN 9780374305505 (hardcover)
Subjects: | CYAC: Best friends—Fiction. | Friendship—Fiction. | Sexual
    abuse—Fiction. | Cape Cod (Mass.)—Fiction.
Classification: LCC PZ7.A1587 (ebook) | LCC PZ7.A1587 Su 2017 (print) |
    DDC [Fic]—dc23
LC record available at https://lccn.loc.gov/2016058780

Our books may be purchased for promotional, educational, or business use. Please contact
your local bookseller or the Macmillan Corporate and Premium Sales Department at
(800) 221-7945 ext. 5442 or by email at MacmillanSpecialMarkets@macmillan.com.

For my family

The Summer of Owen Todd

ONE

You'll hear things about me and Sean Huff. Whispers. Rumors. Lies. Weird talk you won't understand. I get it. There will be stories and half stories for a while. People are people.

Sean was my friend. My best friend. And sure, he isn't my friend anymore, but probably not for any reason you might come up with.

Shay, which is what I call him sometimes, and I got along like brothers from the very first. From the day of the Ping-Pong ball, the coffee cup, and the blood.

We were six, March of kindergarten, waiting for our moms in after-school. I didn't know Sean yet, and I didn't normally go to after-school, but it was weeks before my sister, Ginny, was born, so probably my mom was at her doctor. Anyway, the room was crowded with short chairs and round tables and buckets of blocks, stacks of coloring books, art easels with giant pads, cardboard building bricks. I'm just sitting there at a low table, drawing on a random pad and eyeing the clock over the head of Mr. Davis, a third-grade teacher, dying for my mom to come, when this kid with short brown hair and skinny arms sitting crisscross applesauce on the floor in front of the teacher's desk dips his hand in a yellow beach pail next to him and stirs.

I can't see what's in the pail, but it clatters softly.

The kid has this sly look on his face, and while he's stirring he wiggles his eyebrows at me as if to say, *"Well . . . ?"*

I frown. With my face I say, *"Well . . . what?"*

He does the eyebrows again, then pulls his hand from the beach pail, and he's holding a Ping-Pong ball between his fingers. With a big grin, he tosses it at my head. I swat it away. It dribbles to the floor.

"Enough of that, Sean," Mr. Davis says, not lifting his nose out of whatever he's reading at his desk.

But it's not enough, not for this kid—Sean. He stifles a laugh and pulls a second ball from the beach pail. You have to understand that Mr. Davis can't really see Sean because he's on the floor squirreled up in front of the desk.

Well, this time I'm ready. I swing my drawing pencil back and forth like a baseball bat.

He pitches. I swing. It connects.

The ball soars up, over Sean's head, over the top of the desk, and right into Mr. Davis's coffee cup.

Coffee spurts, the teacher howls, and Sean bellows, "Hole in one!"

"That's the end of that, you two!" Mr. Davis shouts.

But it's still not the end.

Because Sean scrambles over to me on his knees and high-fives me with both hands. Since I'm still holding my pencil, I high-five him back with one hand, which goes between his two and smashes his nose, bloodying it, at the exact moment his mom and my mom walk into the room.

While Sean laughs and his lips and chin drip with blood, the screaming of the moms begins. This goes on for a while. Then, just before his mother takes him home, I beg my mom to have more babies so I can be in after-school more, and the laughing of the moms begins.

Since then, it's pretty much been a done deal between Shay and me, and a lot of good stuff happened after that, but it wasn't all fun. Maybe because of the way we met, the blood thing, you can see our lives together as a series of times we got banged up in one way or another.

In second grade, when we were eight, I was fooling around on my bike to cheer him up while his broken arm was healing when I fell off and sprained my ankle. In

May near the end of third grade, he was diagnosed with diabetes and I nearly died of wasp stings. We were nine then. For years he's had a faraway dad. There had been problems at home, and then his father moved away. Nothing like that for me, but for weeks when my grandfather was dying my mom lived with my grandma, and home without Mom was like having half a family.

Shay and I were also both born in February, so we were a couple of the oldest kids in each grade. He's still kind of skinny and small for our age—I'm taller by three inches.

He was—is—so much smarter than me, it's sometimes scary.

We did everything together, played whole long days by ourselves and cut across the six blocks between our houses pretty much every afternoon, until we didn't.

I guess it's not too much to say Sean still hates me for what I did. I used to cry about that, about the things he said to me, the words he threw at me. I still do. I don't mind saying I cry. Tears aren't everything or even anything. But it's better this way.

At least he's alive to hate me.

TWO

"Are you seriously getting taller?"

I laugh. "No. I don't think so."

It's the second Saturday of June, eight in the morning. The day has opened bright and big and warm and still.

"Yeah, you are. You can probably see the Great Wall of China from up there."

After the cold wet spring, summer has finally come to Brewster. It's "moved in bag and baggage," as my grandmother says. She once told me summer "has plopped its rosy-red bum" down on our long beach, "and ain't getting up for nobody, no how." Grandma is not for beginners.

"I don't feel taller," I say.

"You could be lying."

"True."

So. Brewster.

If Cape Cod is in the shape of your left arm bent at the elbow, with your hand and fingers curled at the tip, you can find Brewster between the bicep of Dennis and the inside elbow joint of Orleans. Sean and I have lived our whole lives here.

"No. I mean it." He skims his flat hand from the top of his head to the tip of my right ear. "Is this even legal?" He makes a face, looks me up and down, and groans. "I thought you were my friend."

We've just come out onto the baseball field behind the Fish House, a restaurant my parents and his mom go to mostly without kids. Coach called an "emergency" practice before our game later that morning—"emergency" because we played like babies the last two games, not hitting, and missing or dropping all the pop flies, flubbing the grounders—not the ones to me, of course, but all in all, we stank.

Our moms dropped us at the field and fled, probably for coffee. They've been friends since the Ping-Pong ball incident. It's like we're all bonded by Sean's bloody nose.

Because of the summer tourist swarm—*plague*, my grandmother calls it—natives get crazy busy on the Cape helping all the strangers relax. From Memorial Day to Labor Day there's no rest for grown-ups, which I guess is one reason for what's going to happen this summer. Most people think Cape Cod is not real, that it's just restaurants and beaches and summer theater, but that's only because they come and go and don't see anything. Real stuff happens here.

Just now there are lots of squeaking, slamming doors, and some cars drive off, raising dust, while some stay parked at angles to the field, spirals of sunlight blooming on their hoods.

I stretch my arms, wiggle inside my T-shirt. It's not tight, but not loose, either. "Everything still fits, I guess. My sneakers, my pants. My mom says I'll get another inch soon, though. Maybe more."

My mother actually does believe I'll grow this summer, as if I've been holding my breath all the way through fifth grade and will finally let go. At the Memorial Day parade two weeks ago, she said I was "*so* poised" for a "growth spurt" and would gain an inch or two soon. She puts on a sad smile when she says things like that. I guess it means I'm growing up? I don't know. I keep stretching, but I don't feel it coming.

"And what's the air like up there?" Sean asks.

"Ha. I think the Fish House just got a delivery."

He sniffs. "I smell rain."

You have to understand. The Cape is a narrow strip of land, an island, really, and, despite what my grandma says, weather doesn't stay all that long. The air can be dry and clear and the sky as blue as blue glass, all for an incredible moment. Then things can change. Like right now, for instance. Behind the field to the west is a band of trees whose tops stand almost frozen against the blue, but over their bushy heads I see shadows of cloud.

I set the bat bag against the end of the bench that sits alongside the first-base line, but the bag slides loosely to the ground and the bats clink and ping as they settle.

Shay slumps onto the bench. "I seriously might be losing height. They're gonna bounce me back to Eddy in the fall."

Eddy Elementary is for Brewster kids, third to fifth grade. Once school lets out on Thursday we'll head over to Nauset Regional Middle in September for sixth.

"You know, right? That my aunt moved?" he says. "Well, she did and two seconds later my mom goes out and finds me a . . ."

Kyle Mahon trots by, says, "Hi. You guys okay? Ready to win?"

We answer, "Yeah," and "Or something," and he slips a bat out of the bag and hustles, laughing, to home plate, where the coach is tossing balls out to the fielders.

I never aimed for that coffee cup, of course, and I couldn't do it again if I tried, but baseball is one of only two things I do even half well. Not as good as Kyle. He can play any position on the field, is a solid hitter, and is the only reason Coach doesn't quit and move away, which he's told us, like, a hundred times he would do if Kyle weren't on the team. Me? I can field all right, but I really love how slow the game is, as quiet and lazy as church on the hot Sundays in August. Standing crouched under the sun, not moving, anticipating the pitch, your feet planted in the grass of the field, looking around, waiting, watching with your shaded eyes, all of which is, face it, most of what anyone ever does in baseball—that's when time almost stands still.

Almost.

Then something happens.

"What did she get you?" I ask. "Your mom. What did she get you?"

Sean shakes his head, grumbles. "Never mind. It's freakish."

I glance at the batter's box. Kyle is swinging slowly as he waits for the ball. He has such good form, steady and natural. There's more waiting. The kid pitching, he's new to the team and stretching his neck from side to side, loosening up or pretending he is, taking his time.

We have a minute before the coach calls either of us to the plate.

"Tell."

"A babysitter," he says.

"A b-b-b . . . that *is* freakish. What do you need a sitter for? Are you pooping in your pants again?"

He makes a sound, blowing out a fruity breath between his lips.

"My mom got a job running a shop in P-town"—what we call Provincetown, about an hour away at the curled fingertip of the Cape—"a pretty great job. She's been looking forever. Your mom must have told you. They talk a lot."

They do.

Mrs. Huff is a tall lady, short jagged hair, always kind of hovering over Sean, nervous, I guess, distracted, and doesn't smile all that much. She worked a long time as office secretary at Monomoy High School, which was good because she had the summers and afternoons off, but she left there a few months ago. She still always dresses like she's going out. Not like my mom, who's much more slowgoing and artsy and isn't nervous at all and is always hugging Ginny and me, which I guess I could use a little less of.

I shrug. "I don't think my mom told me."

"So since my Aunt Karen moved and because of Mom's new job and my 'you-know,' she says she had to find a 'responsible individual' right away to torment me."

Sean's "you-know" is his diabetes. He wears an insulin pod attached usually to his side under his shirt or sometimes on his arm like a jogger's iPod. It's small. He also has to prick his finger to check his blood sugar a few times a day and sometimes adjust the pod to shoot more or less insulin to compensate for what he's going to eat. He can do pretty much anything anyone else can, and you'd never know except sometimes his breath is sour, sometimes fruity. That's part of it.

I think back. His aunt has sat for him since his dad moved out and when his mother had to work late at the high school. I guess this new job means his mom won't be around as much. This will be the first time he's had a regular sitter who wasn't a relative.

"A sitter," he grumbles. "A *baby*sitter. Which they really need to come up with a better name for." He stomps his feet in the dust under the bench. He's mad, but who wouldn't be? He's eleven, basically in sixth grade.

I try to be funny. "*Watcher*, maybe. Or a *handler*?"

"*Handler*, ick. I do like *servant*," he says. "I could go with that. Oh, servant, fetch me that thing."

"So who's the lucky sitter? A nice high school girl?"

"Don't I wish. No. His name is Paul. A grown-up guy. Paul Landis*sss*." He hisses out the name with a slither. "My mom met him at church, interviewed him and everything." Old Sailors Church is where both our families go.

"A church guy. Not the deacon with the wart! Is he crusty old? Like a grandparent? What old man wants to be a sitter?"

"No, he's young. Ish. Older-brother type. Out of

college. You've probably seen him at church. He has a girlfriend. He's okay, I guess. She had me meet him, but it was mostly them talking so, you know, whatever. Mom has to quit the choir because the new job has real long hours. He's some kind of student, taking night courses somewhere, so he has plenty of time. He used to be an EMT and saved somebody's life."

"Maybe he can save you from choking on sugar cubes."

"Funny, really. I told her please get a high school girl. I promised her nothing's going to happen, that I'm saving myself for marriage. That's a joke. She didn't like it. 'No,' she said, 'I'll be gone for hours sometimes, and someone has to see you do your stuff right.'" Sean snorts. "As if I don't know how after three years."

It's actually only two. It was third grade when he was diagnosed. We'd been running around at recess and when we went inside he suddenly got all wobbly. The next thing you know, he nearly crashed into a wall, said, "I feel . . . I feel . . ." went white, and started throwing up in the hallway. A teacher said, "I'm calling your mother!" Sean threw up again outside the nurse's office when I got there with him.

"Sorry," I say. "That's tough."

"Eh. The sitter's a little bit of a chubbo. Plus he does a lot with coffee hour at church, sets it up and stuff."

"Which is maybe how he became a chubbo?"

Shay laughs. "You're lucky you don't need a watcher."

True. When my grandpa was sick, my mother cut down to part time at the newspaper—she did the arts calendar and wrote articles about concerts. She quit altogether when he was dying and hasn't started up again, though she keeps talking about it. She liked it there. Now, she makes crafts that she sells and does volunteer work at a couple of places. Besides, my grandmother watches me and my sister, Ginny, when no one else can. Grandma drives from Hanover, where she lives. It's over the bridge a little more than an hour from here. Ginny's five. Mom promises I can start sitting for her after I turn twelve.

"You could come to the track tomorrow after church," I tell him.

The track.

Go-karting is the other thing I do well. My father and my Uncle Jimmy own J&D Karts in Harwich, and it's the longest running track on the Cape. In summer the business triples, quadruples even. The first few days after Memorial Day it's all right for the natives. You can usually get in a few races. Then the plague begins. It's all tourists until Labor Day. Cape Cod is built on holidays.

"I can't," he says. "I'm actually going to church with the guy tomorrow. It's already all set up. Then my mom wants me to do yard work. Great, huh? Church *and* chores? It'll be my first time with this strange dude and none of it will be fun and I'm going to be with him all day long. 'With Paul.' She says it like that."

"With Powl," I mock. "Powwwwl."

He snorts a laugh. "Yeah. Powwwwl Landi*sssssssssss* . . ."

THREE

Old Sailors Church is a tall, white wooden structure a little down Route 6A from the Fish House.

I have to say, we don't go to church all that often, and it's already planned that Dad and I will go to the track on Sunday, so it's probably a surprise to everybody, even Ginny, when I ask if we can squeeze Old Sailors in before we go. I want to take a look at this new guy, and because of Mom, Dad can never refuse to go to church, even if it means getting to the track a bit later, so we go.

In the car on the way, I tell them about Sean and his babysitter.

"I'm so glad Jen has a full-time job, a good one," says Mom.

"I know Paul," my dad adds as he drives into the church lot. "He does coffee hour, doesn't he? Owen, we can't really stay for that."

"I know," I say. "After communion, zip, we go."

"Ginny and I will get the full scoop before we walk home," Mom says.

Ginny grins. "Scoop? Ice cream? At the General Store?"

"That, too."

When we do get to church, it's late, and the first reading is just over. I give a little wave as we pass Sean, who's in a back pew. He raises his hand like a gun to his head, smiles a fake smile. I want to check out the man kneeling next to him, but his face is buried in the prayer book, and I have to follow Ginny and my mom to catch up with my father, who's scooted up front. Dad thinks that by rushing into our seats, we'll somehow get out earlier. Never mind that right after communion he and I'll slip out, anyway.

A hymn starts. "Holy Spirit, Font of Light." The organ is big, but the choir's pretty thinned out. Mrs. Huff is a strong soprano, but she's not here, and a few of the other good singers are already rehearsing in shows— summer stock is big on the Cape—so the hymn is pretty ragged.

We shake hands at the Peace, but stay in our seats, so

nothing happens until communion. Sean comes up with the last people on his side, and I go up with the first on my side, so I'm close enough to sneak ahead of a couple families and kneel next to him.

He's alone.

"Where's you-know-who?" I whisper to Sean when Ginny plunks down between us.

"You skipped ahead!" she says wetly in my ear.

"Shh," I say as Sean and I take our hosts from the warty deacon's chalice, place them in the palms of our right hands.

"Filling coffeepots," Shay says. He leans over after the deacon passes. "Last chance to bust this party up. Paul has me on doughnut patrol. I can't eat doughnuts! The guy's totally trying to kill me."

Ginny raises her flattened hands between us and pretends to pray. "You're not supposed to talk!" The priest is there now with a chalice of grape juice. I dip the host. He doesn't offer Ginny the chalice, but blesses her instead. Sean dips. We get up, our hands folded.

"I have to go to the track now," I whisper to him.

"Win a race for me."

"And me!" says Ginny.

And that's it.

Shay slips out to the hall to begin patrolling the doughnuts, and I wait for Dad in the rear of the church. The choir is wandering around some new tune I can't identify. Dad hustles toward me, nodding us out to the car.

"Leaving church makes you feel good," he says as he breathes in the warm morning air. "Leaving early, I mean. Don't tell Mom that."

I laugh. "Never."

Even before we get in the car, he starts whistling softly, old songs I don't know the names of, with this wheezy kind of hissing Mom doesn't like, but it means he's happy. He loves summer at the track as much as I do.

When we arrive at J&D's, there are already a couple of kids from the high school rolling out the karts, hanging the OPEN banner, kicking traffic cones into position, generally setting up for the day. The track opens later on Sundays than other days, but it's still early, just before ten. Dad hops into the office, where my Uncle Jimmy is opening the cash register.

I feel a little guilty not having Shay with me. A little guilty, but not a lot. I mean, I used to invite him more often, but he'd have to say no because his mother doesn't like the track. Last summer when she brought him and he spent time in the garage with me, someone swiped his controller (maybe thinking it was a mini tablet), and she's certain it was one of the Monomoy boys who work there. When Sean's pod ran out, the alarm wouldn't stop without the controller, and he had to use a backup pen to inject more insulin. It was a mess. Sean's mother completely freaked, imagining how easily he might have passed out, which I guess he could have. She took him home and won't let him come back.

The truth is, I like it better being at the track by myself. It's me and my dad's place, and the couple of times Sean did race, he was not the greatest driver. He was timid in traffic, and traffic is the best part for me. He was too shy to overtake and just cruised around the outside instead of charging in at the corners.

Even if he were a better driver, it's not like Sean and I can spend too much time on track anyway. When my dad is really hustling and the line of customers doubles up and weaves around before getting to the gate, I spend hours doing nothing but spritzing the seats of the double-seated cars used by parents and their small kids.

I was "volunteered" to do that last summer after a lady complained she sat in pee. She freaked out. Then one of the high school boys laughed and said, "At least it's kid's pee and not old-man pee." And she shrieked louder. Dad had to refund her the drive, and cleaning seats instantly got added to my job description. Dad pays me, of course, but what's minimum wage for pee detail?

Still, the track is my place.

I love the smell of the gas and oil on a warm day, and the sputtering roar of the motors, how each kart has its own sound. I love to work the pedals and feel the fat steering wheel in my hands and the motor throbbing my back as I roar around the track. Whenever I can, I pick number seventeen, since it's the fastest of the karts and even faster when I drive it. On a really hot day, the noise and the smell and everything are even better.

Of course, my dad lets me race for nothing, driving a bunch more laps than usual, but only if paying customers haven't taken all the karts, and on "good days" in the summer there are customers pretty much wall-to-wall, so "good days" aren't that good for me.

The J&D track is a slightly lopsided oval, with one end a shade tighter than the other. It sweeps a little upward from the parking lot, too, but hardly at all. I keep telling Dad they have to put in a real right-hand turn. An oval is the least fun kind of track you can have besides a circle, and it gets boring always turning left. One right-hand turn gives you two more chances to pass, if you twist the wheel properly.

But my dad says why build new track when business is solid? Plus the karts have to be serviced and updated or retired all the time to keep in competition with Wareham and indoor tracks. Wareham *does* have right- and left-hand turns but it isn't on the Cape, even Ginny knows that, though the people who run it like to think they are. Indoor racing, with lights and air-conditioning, racing without weather or sunshine or breezes, isn't real karting, just oversize slot-car racing.

But never mind. There isn't going to be a right-hand turn in my lifetime. Dad loves the noise and the smell as much as I do, probably because he grew up the same way I did, loving karts from day one, and he's also sort of convinced himself that he's essential to J&D and has to be there forever.

"I guess I'm a pretty good manager," he said the other day over breakfast.

"Daddy's the best of anybody!" Ginny said, grinning at him. "Yay, Daddy!"

"Fishing for compliments much?" my mom said.

He laughed. "All I'm saying is that when business is good, it *is* good."

And it's good Sunday after church, too.

I'm there for two and a half, nearly three solid hours, when my dad says, "We've been here since ten, and I don't see any slow time for the next hour plus. Why not run over to the Star and get us something to eat?" He nods

23

across the road, then draws his wrist over his sweaty forehead and adjusts his sunglasses. "Hang out in the AC if you want. I would."

"Really?"

The Star Market is a grocery superstore across the street, separated from the track by the road from Brewster. There's a crosswalk and everything, but my dad's never asked me to go over there alone before.

"Unless you want to wait an hour until your Uncle Jimmy gets back from the hardware store and I can take a break?" Because my uncle's often there first, he tends to pop out a lot during the day. He's older, so maybe he's tired of being there? I don't know. He used to be married but isn't anymore.

"I can do it," I say.

My parents, or one of them, or someone else's, like Sean's mom when she's around, are usually always nearby and herding us along. "You're only in fifth grade," Mom says. And the Star is a place with lots of strangers and far to go out of anyone's sight, which I would be for a while. I mentally go through the walk over, the ordering, the buying, the hanging out in a chilled store. I'm a fan of the idea.

I repeat: "I can do it."

"Here's a twenty. I'll watch you as far as I can from the track." He hands me his phone. "The office number is on here. I'll run over if you need anything."

"I won't."

"I'll have a bottled water and a tuna fish on rye, lettuce, tomato, with a slice of white American." He always orders cheese on his tuna fish sandwiches.

"Got it," I say, already taking a step toward the road.

I did try cheese and tuna once. Dad didn't force me to. I didn't care for it, the flavors didn't blend for me. No, not the flavors, the textures. But maybe I'll try it again. Cheeses are different in different stores.

He goes back into the office as the next race starts. I check both ways. A brick-paved crosswalk goes from our parking lot to the market's. The traffic is thick but slow, and as the summer revs up everybody gets pretty cautious anyway. There are just so many pedestrians, joggers, and dog walkers everywhere you look, not to mention all the extra cars, that drivers pretty much have to take it slow. I make sure everyone sees me. I trot to the other side. Phase One accomplished.

The light in Cape Cod is different from any other place I've been. And I've been all over New England. New York twice, Florida, once. You don't realize how special it is until you drive to the mainland, then return. It's like someone peels a layer of bandages off your eyes. The minute you cross back over the Sagamore Bridge you feel you've been living in black and white, and now life is back in color again. Hopper caught the light, my mom says.

Edward Hopper was a painter who lived here years ago. But right now the light is too bright and white and perfect and heating up the Star Market parking lot to think about anything else but today.

I'll save thinking for tomorrow, the last Monday of the last week of the last grade I'll be in elementary school.

It's a straight shot between the lanes of parked cars. I look back every ten seconds or so to see if my dad is watching me, then I cut across the final spots and enter the store into a wash of cool air, the smell of pickles and pastry, the rumble of grocery carts, and a scratchy song on the sound system.

Since I've usually gone in the Star with my dad, I don't really know my way around the aisles, but I remember that deli counters are often at one end or the other of the store. After only one wrong guess, I find it! I take a ticket, wait till my number's called, and order our sandwiches. I decide to try cheese on mine, too, which makes ordering simple.

"Really, cheese and tuna?" the deli girl says.

"You should try it," I say. She winks at me.

I wait at the counter until she's done making our lunches, then I wander a bit to find the bottled waters.

The phone buzzes. I answer. It's Sean. "Hey," I say. "Wait—how did you—"

"I called the track. Your dad gave me the number."

"Stalker," I say. "What's up?"

"Any fatalities yet?"

"What?"

"At the track?"

"Ha. No. Not at the deli counter, either. I'm in the Star across the street. Alone, by the way."

"I know. Your dad said."

Then I look around. "And in the lady-products aisle, for some reason. I think I'm lost."

"I don't know what those things are for," he says.

"Are you still home? With Powwwwl?"

"Listen." His voice goes very soft. "He left the bathroom door open."

He left the bathroom door open.

So?

Then I get it. "Oh . . . pewwww!"

Sean scuffles his fingers over the phone, whispering. "Not that. He was peeing."

I try to process. "Either way, I'm not cleaning it up for you—"

"With his pants all the way down to the floor."

I freeze. "What?"

"Yeah. I saw everything."

I shiver. "Uck, Sean, gross. Did he leave the door open by mistake?"

He snorts into the phone. "He looked right at me, just holding it."

Bugs come from nowhere and crawl all over me. "Holy crow. What'd you do?"

"I pretended not to see. It was so disgusting. Not to mention he was like a forest. I gotta go. I want to throw up."

The call ends, the phone goes silent in my ear, I stand frozen in the aisle. Really. Frozen. I try to push the soles of my feet hard against the floor so I won't fall over. Then I notice for the first time two high school girls standing behind me.

One of them is giggling to the other. "Wrong aisle for you," she says.

"Sorry."

I pocket the silent phone and I stumble on, still searching for water.

FOUR

School ends Thursday in an explosion of kids running for buses and cars.

Sean yells like a warrior—"Fifth grade is over!"— whooping and wailing his spindly way past me at the final bell. The parking lot is a riot of crisscrossing kids and blowing car horns that don't stop until the principal runs out, red in the face but smiling, and yells something that no one hears, then waves his arms to direct traffic.

When Shay and I dive into the back seat of his mom's minivan, he commands her, "Mother! Get us home STAT! We need to change and get out in this day! As soon as we can! Or we will all die!"

"Yes, sir!" She salutes in the mirror and edges into the line of creeping cars. It's pretty slow in the lot, like all street traffic is getting to be. I have a mental flash of overscooped ice cream cones and slow ball games and fast karts and lying around on the beach. Sean's mom sings silly songs—so completely unlike her I wonder for a second if she's been taken over—for the normally ten-minute drive to my house, which takes twice as long because of the time spent oozing through the packed streets.

It's been four days since the naked-peeing incident.

By now, what Shay told me—and I'm only just beginning to forget the image of the babysitter's eyes staring out while he stands over the toilet—seems more a weird accident than anything else, maybe to Sean, too. He hasn't brought it up again. I find myself thinking—was Paul Landis smiling when he was in the bathroom standing like that? But it's three icky seconds that will get a whole level ickier if I ask Sean that, so I don't. I guess he doesn't tell anyone else, either. It doesn't seem like his mother knows. No, of course she doesn't. She wouldn't be singing songs. Maybe Sean doesn't think it's anything, after all. I let it go, too.

———————

The next morning my dad wakes me up early. "Bus is coming! You're late!"

"Oh, jeez!" I jump out of bed. I stop. "Dad, come on! School's over!"

"Oh. Is it?" He grins. "Seriously, get dressed. Karts."

"But it's my day off. You promised me a couple of days of nothing. I need to do nothing." I slump back onto my bed. It's still warm. I feel a magnetic pull.

"Oh, well, too bad. I need a test driver. But if you're not interested, I'll ask Sean if he wants to come with me." He starts to walk out.

"What? Wait. Test driver for what?"

He grins again. "I'm thinking of buying a kart off a guy in Chatham. I'm driving over to check it out. I thought you liked racing and all, but if you'd rather sleep—"

"I'm up! I'm up!"

―――――――

I throw on my clothes, call Sean, and within ten minutes my dad is swinging by his house in the pickup. Dad's assured Sean's mother that it's a field trip and not a day at the track, so she's okay with it. Shay leaps off his porch and bounces in the front with his backpack, yelping, "Thank you, Mr. Todd. Mom had already asked my sitter to the house, but had to call him off. It was sweet, listening to that. I think maybe he cried. Ha!"

"Really, you don't like him?" my dad says, giving Sean an odd look.

I half wonder if Shay's going to spill the beans about

the pee thing, but his face shows no sign of it. Instead, he says, "You know what Paul told my mom and me? He said he broke his shin when he was small and it got infected. He was in the hospital for weeks and they were talking about cutting his leg off. He was scared, he said. My mom got all teary, and he nearly cried when he showed me the scar later."

"I'll bet," my dad says, pulling out on the street.

"That's pretty ick," I say.

Sean nods. "At least he's okay now. Let's drive!"

And that was pretty much that. Paul Landis was okay now.

———————

The guy selling the kart lived in an old ranch house down a piney dirt road off one of the routes outside Chatham, the elbow-tip of the Cape. His place backed onto a scrappy little pond called Blue Pond.

Even before we swing into his dirt driveway, I spot not one, but three old karts on a side patch of lawn, lined up side by side like used cars. One is barely there. It has no wheels, no seat pad, no steering wheel, no roll bar, and at least one bent axle. The one next to it, a pale green wreck, seems more or less intact, but might be a hundred years old and is all dented and rusty, though it might be mined for parts. The third, however, is a racer. It's dark blue, grimy and spattered with dirt, and the motor is black with caked-on oil, the tires worn to nothing, but you can tell even as it sits there that it has teeth.

"Dad . . ."

"I see it. Don't gawk all over it. I do all the talking, please."

"Yes, sir." I glance at Sean as we get out, slipping my J&D baseball cap on my head. "Ditto for you."

"What's the big deal?" he whispers.

"The blue one looks very good. We shouldn't let on."

"Like I know karts. I should eat a snack anyway."

Sean doesn't eat at regular times. I mean, he does, but he has to eat at other times, too, to keep his blood sugar at an even level. Watching him now, opening his kit, see-ing the pricker thingy to stick his finger with, the check strip, the controller, all that, I get that his mom wants an adult around. Paul Landis, being an EMT, or an ex one, seems a smart choice. Sean checks, nods, takes a fruit bar and a can of tomato juice from his backpack. He's been doing this for two years. I guess it either becomes so rou-tine, or it always annoys you that you have to do it.

Dad talks with the guy for a bit, then calls me over. They start up the motors of both working karts. I slip into the junky green one and Dad gets the dirty hot one. We take them around a small dirt track circling the backyard of the house, and it's clear we were right. I'm barely able to keep up, everything is rattling on mine, one wheel is loose, and Dad's holding way back. After a couple of laps, I'm dragging farther and farther behind until Dad nods and we pull in. The man is watching from his back step. Sean's sitting there munching a carrot. He says something, and the man responds by leveling his hand straight out. It's shaking. I hear, "Can't fix karts. Can't do anything." Sean nods, pulls up his shirt a few inches. "Pod. All the time."

"Switch?" I say to my dad.

We do. I slide into the seat of the blue kart, the pad warm from my dad. The motor sputters powerfully behind me. I press lightly on the gas, and the kart jolts ahead. Trigger pedal. I ease off and start slow. The track is packed dirt and not big, but it's flat and isn't a simple oval, so I get to put the kart through a bunch of turns and one not-too-short straight with a kink in it. Dad is struggling behind me like I did behind him. I slow, speed up, slow to let him catch me. The fun is in the scramble. In the second lap, I don't lift off the pedal though. It's too much for me not to test what it can do, and it does a lot, roaring into a pair of turns without any drift in the back at all.

The old gummy steering wheel feels fat and powerful in my hands, and every time I turn it fast, my insides sway.

This is probably the fastest kart I've ever driven, really balanced. I love it. I want it. Dad has to buy it.

We slow and stop. Dad steps back, studies the good kart back to front. The other one is coughing thick blue smoke.

"This is faster than number seventeen, Dad," I whisper. "Forget the other two."

"Oh, I know, believe me. Now comes the sticky part. I don't like how he had all three lined up like that. I only want this one." He saunters up to the back step and starts talking to the guy.

I follow Sean to the pickup, where he pops his backpack on the floor. "The dirty blue one is really fast," I tell him. "I hope we can get it."

"Is three thousand dollars a lot?" he asks.

"Three thousand? That's what he wants for it?"

"No, for all three. You have to buy them all. Package deal."

"All three? No way. One is great, but the others are wrecks. Maybe for parts. But not for three thousand."

"That's what everybody says, but he told me the cars belonged to his grandkids, who he says he never sees anymore. He wants them all racing again but nobody's willing to rebuild the junky ones and if they say they are he can tell they're lying. I think he likes playing the cranky old man. Say you'll race them all. I bet he'll drop the price."

"He told you that?"

"Not exactly, but I think that's what he wants. Tell him you'll put it in writing."

I look over. My dad's shaking his head. "Dad never breaks contracts."

"So try it."

I frown at Sean, then join my dad, who's saying, "I seriously only want the one. But I'll take the other two for parts if I have to. A thousand, total."

It's the old man's turn to shake his head. "I thought you were a mechanic. Sorry, no deal."

"I am a mechanic, that's how I know how much they're worth," Dad says, exasperated. "Maybe even a thousand is too much."

I turn to look at Sean. He wiggles his eyebrows.

Flipping my J&D cap off and twisting it back on for effect, I say, "You know, Dad, the green one's slow but there's something interesting about it in the turns. And the third one, well, it's a rebuild, but who knows. It could be something again. You're the best kart man on the Cape. Off the Cape, too." I'm talking like a veteran kart mechanic from way back. "I think we could rebuild and race them all."

Dad practically laughs in my face. "Race them? All three of them? Owen, I don't have three thousand dollars for this. I can get brand-new ones for less."

"Not like my Jenna's," the guy says, playing the old man, like Sean said. "The blue one used to be Jenna's." He even gets a faraway old-timer look in his eye, like he's remembering some distant memory from years ago. I almost expect him to shed a tear.

Dad screws up his face. "Sure, maybe not like . . . Jenna's. But I thought since the karts were old, I'd get a better deal."

I butt in. "Draw up a contract, sir, that we'll take them and race them all."

"Owen? Come on. Sorry, sir, I just can't—"

"My dad never breaks a written contract," I say.

The man flicks his eyes over at Sean, then back to my dad. "That true, sir?"

"I'm a man of my word, but a poor man. Sorry, I guess we're going."

"Hold on." The guy looks at me now. "You promise not to cut any of them up for parts, *and race them*, and you put that in writing, you can have the lot for six hundred."

Dad's mouth drops open. He blinks at me, at Sean, at the guy, then fumbles for his checkbook. "Deal!"

It's wrapped up in a few minutes. Dad and the guy, who despite his tremor has got some muscles, hoist all three karts into the back of the pickup, laying the third one, the skeleton, on its side. Dad digs around in the front and comes out with a J&D cap, which the man slings onto his head with a smile. Shay and I climb up into the back and sit in the two working karts—he in the blue one, me in its slower brother. When we get on the road, we wave at the other drivers as Dad passes them, lights blinking. He drives three slow miles to downtown Chatham and parks.

"A celebration," he says. "For Sean, who saved the day."

Shay laughs and wiggles his eyebrows again. "Aw, shucks. Here's to me. And to you, Mr. Todd, since you're gonna have to rebuild those two other karts."

"It'll be a challenge," says my dad. "Could be fun, after all."

Seriously, this is one of the reasons Sean's been my friend so long. He likes having fun, but he knows how to keep a secret and he listens to people. He listened to the guy selling the karts and he figured something out. He's smart about stuff like that. He thinks about what other people are feeling. He's sensitive.

We order fish and chips at the Chatham Squire, and my dad and I get *cheeks*, which sound creepy, but my dad says we're in luck because they're the sweetest part of the fish and not always available. He's right. Lunch is awesome. Sean has broiled cod.

We drop the three karts at the track and head back to Brewster.

"I told my mom to pick me up at your house," Sean tells us, so we pull into our driveway and park. As he climbs out and jumps to the ground, he is as happy as I've seen him for a long time. I think he's happy mostly because he got us such a deal today.

"The first full day of summer vacation is officially *awesome!*" he yells.

And, after a couple of random things fall into place, so is the second.

FIVE

Dad unlocks the side door, which goes straight into the kitchen. Sean and I head to the living room. I hear the refrigerator wheeze open. I check the house phone for voice mail and discover three new messages.

"Maybe my mom?" says Sean.

The first message starts with breathing. It ends with breathing. The next one is just dial tone. The third one coughs, then, "This is Coach. Sorry, I think I just hung up on you. So, no game tomorrow. Too many kids on vacation. No forfeit, since the other team's taking off, too. See you Wednesday afternoon at practice. Three p.m. Uh . . . yeah. That's all." *Click.*

"Yay!" Sean yells. "We didn't lose tomorrow's game!"

"We are awesome at that. But now what? I mean, doesn't that mean . . ."

I don't finish, but "*doesn't that mean*" is the first part of "*doesn't that mean you'll be with your babysitter earlier because your mom'll be at her shop in P-town?*"

And I suddenly have the crazy idea that the first call was from Paul Landis, and his breathing into the phone is also suddenly the creepiest thing I can imagine. I hope it doesn't show on my face, but Sean gets it. He swears under his breath.

Dad enters, eating a cold chicken leg out of a container, though why he's hungry so soon after lunch, I don't know. He offers the container around, and we refuse. "Sean, your mother just phoned my cell. She's on her way."

Then—tumble, tumble—the second rando thing falls into place, only it takes a little while to get to it.

"Why don't you go with her tomorrow," I say.

"Go with who?"

"Your mother. To P-town. Model ladies' dresses and stuff."

He snorts a laugh. "Which I would love to do, but I'll be in the way. Her words. She totally doesn't want me there because the store she says is the size of a closet, so there's no room for me, and she doesn't want me wandering the streets like an orphan. Also her words. I might get abducted by pirates."

"Provincetown?" My dad pretends to think about it. "Abducted. Pirates. Yeah, I can see that."

41

I try to imagine a way Sean can avoid having the sitter. "Or maybe your mom will bend the rules and you can come to the track with us."

"Sorry, no track for us, either," Dad says. "Mommy's driving to Grandma's, which you should know because it's the anniversary of when Grandpa died. So I'm volunteered to take Ginny to dance class. You could come with us. Model tutus." He starts another piece of chicken, his eyebrows doing the questioning as he bites in.

I hear a car coming up the drive to the house. "Well, I haven't been to Provincetown in forever. Maybe I could go with *you*. We could buddy up, keep each other from being kidnapped."

Sean looks at me. I can see him flipping through all the arguments he'd have to have with his mother before he shakes his head. "She won't go for it. She's all business lately. She's kind of . . . worried about this shop. Two kids? Even two kids as awesome as us? There's another side of my mom you don't want to see."

"Ask her," my dad says, tugging open the side door for Mrs. Huff.

She stands outside smiling. "Ready, Sean? Did you have fun?"

I just push right into it. "Can you take Sean and me to P-town with you tomorrow?"

"Come in," Dad says.

She tries to keep smiling as she steps into the kitchen, but I can tell it's hard for her. She runs her fingers through her short hair next to her ear. Her lips tighten. Her eyes flick toward my father, who smiles back at her and offers the container of chicken parts. She shakes her head.

"I'm sorry, Owen. It's not really a great idea."

"But if we go together, I'll keep Sean busy, and he'll keep me busy. We'll take care of each other."

My dad suddenly laughs, which doesn't help, but he sets down the container, pulls open the freezer door, and takes out a can of ground coffee. "Coffee, Jen?"

"Oh, no. We have to get going—"

"Please?" Shay says. "Please, please!"

She seems a bit twitchy, I don't know why. Maybe she's thinking of all the stuff she needs to do and is just nervous. "Sean, I don't think so."

"No, Mom, this is good," he says, whining a little. "You know the store is a big thing to handle. You need moral support. We're it." He points a finger back and forth between us.

"You'll have nothing to do! It's a dress shop. A tiny dress shop for ladies."

"Yeah!" says Sean. "Right across the street from . . . Marine Specialties."

She sighs. "Sean—"

"Owen, it's the coolest store," he says. "They have so

much junk in Marine Specialties. Everything. You can buy a submarine. Seriously. A submarine. No lie."

"A submarine," I say.

"A small one," Shay says.

"But big enough for two, right? I've always wanted one."

Dad laughs again, spoons coffee into the machine. "Jen, you're sure, no coffee?"

"Thank you, no. You're not getting a submarine, Sean."

"Probably not this weekend, I agree," he says. "We have to test drive it first. You always test before you buy. I'm sure we could get a good deal on it, too, if we promise to sail it. Or dive it. No, no. This weekend, we should start small. Maybe some scuba tanks. Or an oar." He laughs. "*Or* . . . an . . . *oar*! Get it? Seriously, Owen needs a break from his family. No offense, Mr. Todd."

Dad laughs more. "I'm fine with it if you are, Jen. I know the marine store. It is pretty fantastic. Owen would love it."

Sean's mother twists up her face now, but there's a glimmer of a smile in there somewhere. "Mm-hmm. I can see a thousand ways this could go off the rails. But I guess . . . if you really, *really* want to. Owen?"

"Yes! Yes!"

Sean starts jumping up and down while his mother groans a long sigh. But she finally breaks out in a full smile. It's a tense smile, but I'll take it. "This is so unlike me. But . . . I'll pick you up at eight, Owen."

"I'll be ready at seven!" I say.

"And I'll still be here at eight."

We slap fives, Sean and I. Single ones.

"Dude, excellent awesomeness," he says, "not one, but two days in a row!"

SIX

Mrs. Huff pulls in my drive at eight a.m. sharp, and when I leap out the door into her minivan I find Shay still grinning like a chimp.

"Everything okay?" I ask.

"Oh, yeah!"

A little over an hour later we're parked in a lot a block away from Commercial Street, the crazy busy shopping street that follows the curl of the giant Cape Cod Bay.

"You boys stick close," Mrs. Huff says as we hustle down to her shop. "You could get lost here and no one would ever find you again." She stops on the street. "Sean, did you bring—"

"I have both pods, Mom. You take one." He hands her a small zip case.

Belle-Teak is the name of the dress shop his mom co-manages.

Shay tells me the name is supposed to be a play on the word *boutique*, but he's not exactly sure how and neither is his mother, because Mrs. Huff's boss, Miranda Something, who owns the store, chose it.

We enter the shop to find Miranda frowning into the register. She's a big, boxy woman and is the one with all the business sense, Sean told me, while his mother, besides working at the high school, used to work in a bunch of stores and even designed dresses when she was younger. Miranda seems all right, but after Shay's mom introduces us, they talk low to each other, and neither seems happy about something. The doorbell bings, and this girl, dressed in a loose black T-shirt, black jeans, and black boots, maybe a college student, pushes into the store like she owns it. I'm ready for someone to tell her we're not quite open, but they both say, "Hi, Gee," so the girl apparently works for them. She responds with a flat smile and a long ragged sigh.

When Sean's mom asks her, "Can you arrange these on the racks outside?" gesturing to a row of flimsy dresses, the girl makes such a slow, whispery, "Sure," I wonder if she'll make it to the door. She looks like she wants to die.

"Owen, when I said it was a tiny shop, I meant it,"

Mrs. H. says. "Maybe you two can . . ." She nods across the street to Marine Specialties. "And no submarines, please. We simply don't have room."

I laugh because his mom doesn't make that many jokes, then I suggest she lend us her cell phone, like my dad did. She loves this idea because it shows how responsible at least one of us is. She shows Sean the store's number and gives the phone to him. We are out the door in a flash, fleeing the shop like we did school on the last day. On the sidewalk we carefully avoid Miss Glum, who is roughly hanging the dresses, but does seem to be arranging them in size order, which I think shows potential.

It must be barely twenty feet across the street to the other shop, but the river of Commercial Street practically drags us away in its current. Even this early, a little before nine thirty, the pavement is jammed with people. There are at least three different songs playing from public speakers. A wolf pack of girls in tight T-shirts squeezes past us, while five or six boys in long shorts lope along behind them. Those poor girls. The guys trailing them are goofily slapping one another. But Shay's eyes are fixed only on the marine store, which is drawing him in like a tractor beam. A low-tide smell mixes with the tang of boat fuel and pastries just before I enter.

Then I enter.

Whoa.

Like Doctor Who's TARDIS, Marine Specialties is so much bigger inside than out I can barely believe it. It's crowded wall to wall, floor to ceiling like a hoarder's museum of every kind of junky stuff you can imagine. Grandma would call it "crazy crap."

"Seriously," I say. "This is the exact opposite of your mother's store."

"You mean Belle-Teak?"

"I do mean Belle-Teak."

"Well, yeah, because . . . holy cow!"

From the ceiling over Sean's head hangs a complete old-fashioned rubbery diving suit. It has an enormous bronze ball of a helmet with a grilled-over glass porthole on the front, showing a sexy lady's heavily lipsticked mannequin head inside. The diver's arms are straight out as if it's flying. Not far from this is what must have been the first surfboard invented. It's at least fifteen feet long and could hold five people. Gawking at it, I nearly fall over and realize we're pinned between tables crowded with stacks of plates and dishes and knives and forks and glasses that you could use to feed thousands.

"What a freaky place," I say when Sean nudges me to look to my left.

Standing there is a bearded old man, staring at us

from among the tables, as motionless as a mannequin. "He looks like he fell down from the ceiling," Shay whispers. "But I think he's actually alive. And he has a man bun!"

The front part of the man's head is bald and scabby, but from about his ears back, these great waves of gray hair are pulled into a knot on the top of his head that looks like some sort of dangerous growth. His long beard is split in the middle like in pictures of Moses. He wears a T-shirt that says "Don't Ask Me."

He shuffles slowly over to us. "Can I help you?"

"But, your shirt . . . uh, no, thanks," Sean says. "Just looking."

"All right," the man says, "all right." Except he doesn't step away so much as stare over our shoulders at the other customers.

We squirm off through the tables.

"I think he thinks we're stealing," I say. "Or going to steal. Or used to steal. I feel his eyes following me."

"His scent is, too. He smells bad."

"It's that man bun. Probably infected." I glance across the street. Miss Glum is still fooling with the dresses. I wonder how much she gets paid.

Sean goes over to a strip of icy blue neon crawling up the wall like a snake, and he touches it. "Warm. Who knew?" I think the snake is supposed to be art for sale, but it's set in the middle of a web of dusty fishing nets, ships' rigging, and buoys made of thick green glass, so it's hard to tell.

Suddenly, Sean's limbs tense, and he stiffens. "Owen. Behold."

I follow his eyes to see the submarine that was foretold to me. It is pretty small, a two-seater, if that, but it has a conning tower, prop blades coming out the back, and fins along the side. It's hung from the ceiling at a diving angle.

"I want it," I say.

"We'll need your dad's pickup, but it should fit."

"I want it."

"Maybe my new best friend, the go-kart guy in Chatham, will let us take it out in his pond."

"I want it."

"Do you want it?"

I turn to him, nodding. "I do."

All in all, we must spend at least two solid hours in the store. The people that run it have got to be used to people just gaping and browsing and not buying anything at all, although some stuff is dirt cheap. There are hundreds of ratty, rusty remnants of junk left over from wars or seriously demented camping trips. Tents, canteens, strings of cartridges, leather bags, gas masks, military knives under glass, hiking sticks, canvas belts, brass boat instruments. There is also a life-size mermaid figurehead from an old sailing ship.

"Dude," I say, "she's got—"

"I see them."

Wooden buoys, tin buoys, baskets, harpoons, lobster traps, lanterns, old street signs, bells, models of ships, barrels, coats, cots, hammocks, cartons. There is even a display of, no kidding, pirate cutlasses. And all the time the gray guy with the smelly man bun is tracking us with his beady, old-man eyes. Finally, I catch sight of someone worming through the racks and tables directly toward us.

I nudge his shoulder. "Your mom."

"Ugh. I know that face," he says. "She's mad. Pretend we're innocent."

"We *are* innocent—"

"Something's wrong," she says sharply, her eyes flicking distractedly at all the junk. "We're missing some money and merchandise. Small stuff, but yesterday's totals are not coming out right. The day before, either. Miranda's on the warpath."

"Is it Goth Girl?" I ask.

"Maybe. Maybe not. There's another girl on weekdays after school. We had a little bit of an argument, Miranda and I, but she'll take care of it. How about some lunch?"

The afternoon drags. Shay and I are in and out of the dress shop. I use my talent at spritzing to go over the front windows. Mrs. Huff beams. Sean sweeps whatever floor space isn't covered with displays and racks, which isn't much. We rest in a couple of metal chairs angled on the blazing sidewalk, watching over the merchandise, the people that go by, the dogs. Finally everyone feels better when Gee clocks out for the day. In fact, Miranda starts whistling, like my dad, only more in tune, and loves how I join her in some of the old songs I picked up listening to him. I think Mrs. Huff is surprised I know so many of them.

By the time we get back to my house, it's just about suppertime. I hop out of the minivan. "Thanks, Mrs. H. That was awesome."

She smiles at me from behind the wheel. "It was."

I lean in Sean's window. "The sub should be delivered tomorrow, so keep an eye out. In the meantime, I'll dream of cutlasses."

"I'm diving for mermaids."

"Sean!"

He laughs. "See ya."

SEVEN

Two excellent days old, and the summer is on track. Literally.

Because the weather is good, the next couple of days I'm at J&D's a lot. On Sunday we skip church and I go straight to Harwich with my dad to clean seats (mostly) and race (only once). Monday the same, until Mom and Ginny swing by with homemade lunch, then bring me home in the afternoon for yard work. Tuesday, I forget. Same stuff? No. Before I get up, Dad's already off to Hyannis to get parts to rebuild the karts we bought, so the rest of us spend a couple of hours at the Brewster Bookstore, where my mom has friends from when she used to handle their publicity at the newspaper.

"It's summer-reading time," the white-haired lady

behind the counter reminds me and Ginny. Mom smiles and says, "Pick something, each of you."

Ginny tears off into the corner with the big floor pillows and sacks out. I spin the racks. She gets a picture book about vampire bats playing baseball, and I find a novel about a boy who disappears. Then food shopping, then Ginny and Mom at ballet. Sean is with Paul all those days. That night he calls.

"We went to a museum," he tells me. "Not a museum with paintings, though. Glass."

"Glass?"

"Glass. Paul's mother collects old glass. Apparently there's glass old enough to put in a museum. They display it behind glass. Silly me. I thought you just throw it away—"

"Or sell it at Marine Specialties."

"But no. People go there to see it. The old glass. She has tons of it, Paul told me. She met us there." Shay's voice is low, not whispering, but shaky.

"You okay?"

"Yeah. He has a limp, did you see that?"

"No."

"It's little. Anyway, it was a regular field trip."

"What's his mother like?"

"She's okay. Nice. Used to be a teacher in Sandwich."

"She probably ate them, too."

"Her students?" Shay laughs. "Yeah. She said she did."

He gets his voice back somewhere during this. "So, you?"

"The usual. Dad's working on the blue car first. I can't wait until it gets on track. Your mom should let you come again. You helped us get it, after all."

"Yeah, maybe."

The first time I actually see Sean after our trip to P-town is at practice on Wednesday afternoon. It's as lazy as usual, no matter how Coach tries to electrify us for the game on Saturday. Except this time, Kyle Mahon drops a bomb.

"I'll be gone for a few days," he announces as we sit on the bench waiting to bat.

"What? No," I say. "Does Coach know?"

"He cried. Seriously. Cried. Now he's mad. The two stages of coaching. But I told him I can't do anything about it. It's my family's summer vacation and they want me to come with them. Odd, I know, but families."

"I wouldn't know," Sean mumbles.

Kyle's face flickers into a frown, then he stands. "Sorry. But what can I do?"

"Not go?" I say. "Where *are* you going, anyway?"

"Virginia Beach."

Sean snorts. "Uh . . . they have those here, you know. Beaches." He points over the trees.

Kyle laughs. "But my parents are high school teachers.

You can't vacation in the same town as your students. Dad in swimming trunks? He'd never get over it."

"That makes strange sense," I say. "It's just for one game, right? Tell me it's just for one game."

"It's just for two games."

"Bury us! We're dead!" Shay says.

Kyle smiles. "Not so much. Owen, you're good in the field. Real good. And Sean, I hereby appoint you my designated hitter."

"I'll be your designated *sitter*," he says. "I've been training for eleven years."

"You've got it down now," Kyle says, chuckling.

"Yeah, *down*," I say. "His butt on the bench."

"Not that it matters, but I may not be here either," Shay says. "I might go to my dad's." His father lives in Connecticut, in the middle of the state somewhere. "He works for Colt, you know."

Kyle shakes his head. "Colt? What is this Colt?"

"Colt. The Colt .45. The handgun that won the Wild West!"

"Scary," Kyle says. "Coach is waving at me. I guess I'm up. Don't want him to weep again. Or froth at the mouth." He trots off to home plate, swinging two bats.

Sean's never really told me what happened at home, but I almost don't remember a time when his dad was living with him and his mother.

"Mom wants me to like my dad, but it's strange," he says. "I think she wants me to like him, but maybe not too much."

"What does that mean?"

He shrugs. "Your guess. I think he's just lonely. He was lonely when he lived with us, too. How, I don't know. I don't really get it, but he didn't get us, either. Maybe that's why, you know, we're all split up."

"Cut the chatter and get over here, everybody!" Coach yells. "I need to talk."

Groaning, we hustle over to home plate.

Coach takes a deep breath before he starts. You can tell that Kyle being out two games has crushed him. "It's going to be an uphill battle these next we—weeks, without—without a full team," he says, barely getting it out. "But then, it's always uphill. And why?"

John Pelosic raises his hand.

"Because you don't care!" Coach shouts, ignoring the hand and getting some steam back. "You just stand there and do nothing while the other team scores!"

I listen, I try to look serious, but I'm not sure Coach has it right.

We care. We do. But we care about other stuff, at least I do. I move on the field. Some. I'm ready to bolt off right or left to scoop up a grounder. But for me, it's the not-moving I really love. Just standing in the grass under the slow gold sun. It's like the air goes still around you, like a skin, and you'll break it if you move. So why would you want to move? It's why I love baseball. Not as much as karting, but nearly. Karting is all about moving. Baseball is all about staying still.

But to Coach, it amounts to not caring. Finally, he claps his hands louder than anyone I've ever heard. "Now, you half on the field. Others on the bench. Kyle, you're up. Pay attention, everyone. Play ball!"

As our half huddles behind and around home plate, Sean returns to the first-base bench. He plunks down at the end, his head in his hands. Glancing at Coach, who's concentrating on Kyle, I trot over.

"Shay, what's going on?"

His answer is to suddenly slide off the end of the bench and fall to the damp grass as if all the air has gone out of him.

"Whoa . . . dude!" I say, laughing.

"Shh." He looks behind me to see if anyone is listening. No one's near. He leans over so his forehead almost touches the ground. Rocking right back up, he says, "Paul was there. Yesterday."

"I figured."

"No. Not yesterday. This was Monday."

I watch him rocking and staring at his shoes. "What was Monday?"

"He's showing me a picture on his phone of a boat he might buy, right? No, wait. It *was* yesterday. Anyway, he's flipping through his photos and 'accidentally' flips past something so gross I can't even tell you."

He's serious. I can see it in his eyes. His lips are pinched in disgust. Coach is still busy. Sitting on the end of the bench, I try to be funny. "What was it? Vomit? Except why would you take a picture of vomit? Was it a dead body?"

He takes a while. His head bobs up and down over his lap. "It was a body," he says softly. "But it wasn't dead. It was naked."

The quiet word cuts the air around the bench.

It's the *k* in the word that cuts, and it hacks into the humid, slow air around us. You just don't say that word outside. I feel as if somebody just stood on my chest. I gulp in a breath, turn to see if anyone hears, but I'm the only one there.

"Why does he have a picture of . . . a person with no clothes on?" Then something tingles in my groin. "Is it a woman? He's showing you naked women on his phone? Completely naked? Was it his girlfriend? Whoa."

He shakes his head. "No. I mean, yes. Completely naked. But no, it wasn't a woman."

"A . . . girl?"

Sean keeps shaking his head. "A boy."

It seems like the bench is shaking under me, but it's

60

me who's shaking. I have to stand up. The bench is suddenly too dirty to sit on. "What do you mean 'accidentally'? You said he 'accidentally' showed you the picture?"

"It was, like, a fraction of a second, but if it was what I think it was, I can't get it out of my head."

"Just like I can't. A boy with no clothes on. What the heck? First naked peeing. Now this? Where was he?"

"Sitting right next to me!"

"I mean the boy in the picture."

I don't even know why I ask, except that I find I need to imagine it. Why? I don't know that, either. "A naked boy doing what? Where?"

His voice is very low, soft. "He was in a room, like a living room. He was lying down on a couch with his face turned away."

"Sleeping?"

"Uh . . . no."

"Where were you when you saw it?"

"Sitting on *my* couch. Paul came over and plopped down and opened his phone. He was all, 'I have to show you this boat I'm thinking of buying,' and he opens his photos, and there it is. He flicks it right away and says, 'Oops, my little brother.'"

"His brother?" I say. "Who knew he had a brother. Is he ever at church?"

"Jeez, I don't know! Then he said sorry about the

other day with the open door. It's no big deal, he said. He said he grew up that way and lots of people do."

"What, they strip down naked when they pee?"

"Shhh!" he says. "I don't know why he has it on his phone for. I couldn't see the kid's face, but he looked like maybe he's in high school. I mean, you could tell. He was older than u-us." He chokes a little on the last word. I can't see Sean's face at all now. He hangs his head low over his lap.

"Sean Huff, you're up next," says the coach, who is hovering by the batter's box with Kyle, who smiles at me and shrugs.

Sean looks up, raises his hand to the coach, but doesn't get up from the ground.

My shoulders turn cold, icy. The skin on my arms itches. Again I feel like I'm covered with insects. "Then what happened?"

Shay wiggles his fingers. "Nothing. He showed me the boat he wants to buy and I went to my room to play a game and then my mom came back and he was gone. That's it."

"Did you tell her? I mean, that's two naked things, right? It's super weird . . ."

He snorts at me. "Do *you* tell *your* mom stuff?"

"I don't know. I guess I tell my dad."

"Leaves me out."

The truth is I don't tell either of my parents everything.

The wasp attack, for example. That was behind the Fish House. I had run out to get something from the car while we were eating, a phone charger maybe, I forget. And, I don't know, I saw this papery nest swinging loose under the eaves, and thought wouldn't it be cool to throw a rock at it like it was a target. It was ragged and just hanging there empty, I thought. Well, the first rock missed and hit the gutter. But the second one didn't. What was I, eight? No, nine. I should have known better. The swarm shot out on me faster than I could run and stung my neck and shoulders and arms. Mom screamed and rushed me to the doctor, while I made up a story about how the nest was on the ground and I accidently stepped on it and wasps attacked me. Only Sean knows that I caused it, and he's never blabbed.

Now he's all sucked into himself and sitting still on the damp ground, not rocking. He looks either like he's going to turn into stone or bolt right off the field into the trees and never come back.

"It's really weird, Shay. You have to tell your mom."

"I'm telling you because I'm not sure. He was flipping through his pictures so fast it was like a fraction of a second. I don't even know what I saw."

"You know what you saw." I listen to myself talking to him like a teacher.

He shrugs. "It was so fast. Plus my mom tried so hard

to get a sitter who could do her exact hours. She needs this job at the shop. *We* need it, she says. She's been out of work for months. I'm not saying anything to her. It's okay. Forget about it. It was a mistake."

I know the coach will call for Sean again, but when I look over he's dancing behind the plate with Austin Wien, showing him a different grip. I try to put it together in my head. Sean's babysitter, Paul Landis, is in charge of coffee hour. He's an EMT. He has a girlfriend and a mother who collects glass. And there's naked stuff going on. I think about telling my dad, but the words don't form in my mind.

How do you say this stuff?

But I remember that I'll be at the kart track with Dad all day again tomorrow and maybe some perfect time will come up and mistake or not I'll think of the right words to say.

Kyle takes the bat from Austin. This is going in slo-mo. Austin has long red hair that curls down and up out of the back of his batter's helmet. Kyle crouches. The ball comes, Kyle swings, and the ball cracks against the bat and flies out to the scrambling fielders.

"Ha! Good one!" Coach calls. "Real good. That's how it's done." Then he glances back at our bench. "Sean Huff, you're up."

But Sean is still folded into himself on the ground next

to the bench. The slats of the bench shadow the back of his shirt. He seems smaller than he usually does.

"I'll take his spot," I call. "Shay, I'll be right back."

He looks up. "Don't tell anybody what I told you. It was probably a mistake."

"You could skip a day with the sitter." I take a bat from the bag next to the bench, swing it around. "Stay with us next time."

"Owen, batter up!"

"Yeah? Tomorrow?" he says. "We could do stuff together. Whatever you want."

"Tomorrow? You're going to visit your dad, aren't you?"

"No, that's Friday. Tomorrow Paul's supposed to come again."

My knees feel like buckling in half. "I really have to help my dad at the track. Will your mom let you come to the track with me?"

He shakes his head. "No. I'm a sick kid, and they steal stuff, remember?"

"Owen Todd, get over here!"

"I gotta go."

"And that's why I need a sitter," he says. "Never mind. Go. I'm fine."

EIGHT

We lose Saturday's game. How could we not? While Kyle's lolling on a foreign beach, we're busy not hitting, dropping balls, and stumbling our way to another loss.

Sean isn't there, either. He stays with his sitter on Thursday and on Friday his mother drives him to visit his father in Connecticut.

He isn't due back until Wednesday at the earliest. I decide not to ask my dad about it until after Shay comes back, because if Shay talks with his own dad about the sitter's smartphone picture, maybe that'll end it.

I formally meet Paul Landis on Sunday. I decide to stay for coffee hour to check him out for real. Mom promises to drive me to the track later.

In the hall after the service, she introduces Paul to me

and Ginny, then goes to get half a bagel and some fruit in a plastic cup. That's always her Sunday breakfast.

After nodding at Ginny, who's not interested and goes after my mom, Paul turns to me, "I've seen you around, Mr. Owen Todd! You're a friend of Sean Huff's, are you not? I'm sitting for him, but you know that."

Are you not? Weird wording.

I read his name from his badge and try not to catch him in the eye. Sean's description wasn't great. The guy's a few years older than just out of college. He's tan, with a round face, sandy hair that needs a comb. He wears chino shorts and boat sneakers and a polo shirt with the church logo on the chest.

"Yes, Mr. Landis," I say.

"Nahhh, none of that *Mr. Landis.*" He draws out the first word like he's a goat. "Call me Paul. I'm not all that old." He laughs and shuffles his sneakers to prove he can dance or something. He's very comfortable with himself, moving and chatting while his eyes flick over the tables, motioning his helpers to tighten up the cookie trays, refill the cream pitchers.

His voice is a casual kind of sound, like leaves in a breeze. I see now he *is* a little pudgy around the middle, but since he's wearing shorts I notice he has hard biker's calves, which makes me think he's sort of athletic. I remember about the leg Sean told me was almost cut off and wonder which one it was. They both look strong. I don't see a scar. All in all, it takes me a few seconds to remember something else about him.

I said before that we don't go to church every week, but his tooth-filled grin this morning reminds me of the pancake breakfast Old Sailors sponsors at the parade every Memorial Day.

There he was, four weekends ago, in his church polo with one cuff rolled up over the shoulder, wearing sunglasses and a goofy *Cat in the Hat* hat, flipping pancakes at the griddles set up on the church lawn the morning of the parade. He was grinning a grin that wouldn't quit. His leafy, breezy voice was booming and laughy, and you could hear him practically over the blare of the marching bands.

"Two plates pronto for Master Mahoney!" "I think you would like some extra bacon, wouldn't you, Miss?" "More syrup for this youngster! He *drowns* his pancakes in syrup, this youngster does, ha-ha!"

The other men seemed to think their leader was awesome. In my memory, he was almost too happy, doing these extra-high flips of the pancakes, catching them on plates, but whatever. Church is like that, ultrahappy sometimes.

Paul Landis's expression that day didn't budge for over

three hours. I know because I was helping my mom in a craft booth a little down the parade route. He never lost his smile except when he had to boss around some kids who helped with supplies. I watched him get mad at two of the high school girls who are in the choir, his cheeks red as a steamed lobster. I remember this because they're pretty and hang out together all the time. But he never got mad at the boys. And the boys—I see John Pelosic and Adam Sisley in my mind, but there were others—barely helped at the breakfast at all. I never saw them bring out more batter from the kitchen or exchange full trays of bacon for the empties on the outside tables or clear or anything like the girls did.

Recalling it now, a month later, I'm not sure what to make of this, only that I remember it.

———————

Finally, people trickle away, and coffee hour ends. Mom drops me at the track.

There are a few people in line, but they aren't being let in yet. I wonder why until I get out of the car, when I'm surprised to hear the high-pitched whine of one particular engine. I run out through the garage, and there's my dad watching my uncle, who's alone on the track, taking the new machine through its paces.

"Dad?"

He turns, grins, and kisses Mom and Ginny, who've come in behind me. "We're waiting for the line to build to a full track. In the meantime, the blue kart is done."

"This is what you bought?" Mom says. "Nice."

"More than nice," I say. "A worthy competitor to number seventeen." Which I'm not sure means anything to her, but I say it mostly to my dad.

"When can I race?" Ginny asks.

"Soon," says Dad.

"Not too soon," Mom adds, putting her arm around Ginny.

The kart has been washed and steam-cleaned of oil and grease, and it looks even faster than before, no slide at all in the corners, which my uncle is taking almost flat out. He slows when he sees us.

"Great buy, Dale," he says to my dad. He kisses my mom, too. "The other ones, well, they'll take time to bring up to this one, but yeah, in time. Right now, this baby's too fast for the other karts, even number seventeen, but maybe we can do something like a special race, the faster cars, the more experienced, older drivers. Charge extra?"

"It's *probably* faster than seventeen," I say, "but I bet the two of them together would be a heck of a race."

Uncle Jimmy laughs. "Bring it out."

I turn. "Dad?"

He grins, heads for the office with Mom and Ginny. "Go for it. Just a few laps. We'll have to open up the gate soon."

I rush into the garage, start up seventeen, strap on a helmet, slip in, and drive onto the track. I take it around once before pulling alongside my uncle. We start moderately, and I can sense he's holding off, toying with me, as we enter the first turn in the middle of the track, me on the outside. Then, as we pull onto the straight, I brake and drop behind him, then quickly steer to the inside. I block him. He has to take a wider line through the next corner. I'm firmly on the inside, and I know I have to jam my foot to the floor and pull out of the turn while still holding the inside line. I do. He's speeding up to go around me on the straight, but I veer out just a little to gain a better position for the upcoming turn. We're wheel to wheel for a half lap, when he outwits me at the next corner. I wiggle back and forth behind him. He turns his head to see which side I'm on, and I dart inside again. I'm about to overtake him when the whistle sounds from the garage, and we have to come in. The customers are filing out into the other cars. I find I've been laughing the whole time, and I realize that I don't want to leave this kart, the track, or Cape Cod ever.

This is me.

The first drivers rush out and jump in the karts as

the two of us putt into the garage. Shaking as I always do after a ride, I take up my post on a stool in the shed and for the rest of the morning watch the races, my bottle of spray cleaner and paper towels ready. Today, I don't even mind. That was real racing. Short, but fast, and a promise of more speed to come. I breathe in the exhaust. I love it.

Around noon, after Mom and Ginny go home, I get a call on my dad's phone. It's Sean. "Hey, how's it going?" I ask, hoping things are okay. "You're still with your dad, right?"

"Yeah. He's actually pretty cool. I'm going on a private tour of his gun factory tomorrow morning. He runs a whole department there."

"Nice."

"Plus, he's so laid back about the whole diabetes thing. Just, you know, like it's no big thing. I mean, I guess I remember him and Mom shouting, but it's sort of crazy how different they are. He cooks, too. Not a huge range of stuff, but decent. Later today we're going to Mark Twain's house."

"The steamboat guy? Maybe your dad'll let you buy one."

"He would. He totally would."

Then I remember Paul Landis. "Hey, have you talked to him about . . . you know?"

"Way to remind me, Owen. No. Not yet. Maybe later. On the steamboat."

There's more, but he hangs up soon after, and I feel that weight lifting again, just a little. I think about my parents. My dad's not fussy, either. Maybe no dads are. Mom is different. Maybe it's the whole getting-taller thing, but I almost think she wants me not to grow. Ginny doesn't mind all the hugging. It's starting to bother me. I hope it doesn't show, but I see Mom sometimes catch herself when she wants to get closer to me. With my dad it's different. *"Go for it,"* he says. *"Race!"*

After a while I walk over to the market for my and my dad's lunch again, adding my uncle's order, too. It's sunny, hot, and noisy trekking across the big parking lot. I know where the deli and the water bottles are. When I get back I race two more times.

It's a go-kart track.

It's Cape Cod.

What's not to love?

NINE

Sean and I leave things like that for the next few days. He doesn't call again. I don't see or hear from him until Thursday night.

It's nearly nine. It's been clear all day, and warm—it's the first week of July now—and the sun's just gone down behind the trees in my backyard. Our patio is green and blue in the twilight. Because the heavy dew soaks them, I'm pulling the cushions off the deck chairs and storing them in the shed when a pebble trills across the patio stones to my feet.

At first, I look up. I don't know why, it never rains rocks. I'm not thinking about Shay. Then another pebble clacks on the flagstones and I scan the hedge along the rear of the yard. Sean shuffles between the bushes and trots over to me.

"Whoa. When did you get back?"

"I have to talk to you," he says.

A cold finger touches my neck. "Yeah?" I don't want this conversation to go sideways, so I come out with, "I raced against the new kart again today, just me and my dad this time. It's fast, but I think number seventeen and me are organic. Ten laps. I won by nearly half a lap. Proving it's totally the driver."

He's not listening. "I have to talk to you."

He's not looking at me, either, but up at my house.

I glance around. The kitchen window is lit; my dad is standing at the sink. I think at first he's alone, and that my mom is upstairs, reading to Ginny, who can't sleep and has a wicked cold I'm trying not to catch. Then Dad turns his head, and I see his lips move. Mom must be in the kitchen with him, sitting at the table. I look up. Ginny's window is dark.

I turn back to see Sean's sidestepped behind the shed and out of the light. I know you can't see well out a lit window at night, but I guess he doesn't want to take the chance that my dad might see him. I don't want to know why.

"What's going on?"

"Around the garage," he says.

We dodge along the side of the garage and stop. I look toward the street. It's in a kind of deep green shadow.

Under the streetlight, the crushed shells covering our driveway are yellow with blue shadows.

"I couldn't look at my mom's face," he says. He's blue in the shadows too, with the light behind him.

"What do you mean? When?"

"When she came home from work today. I couldn't look at her."

"What are you talking about? I thought you were with your dad."

"That ended yesterday when something happened to a machine and he had to go back to work."

"You were back all day today?" I ask.

He shifts from foot to foot nervously. "Remember how I told you when Paul first came to my house he asked me about my room, about if my mother cleans it or I clean it?"

"You didn't tell me that. And if you ask me, it looks like nobody cleans it—"

"The reason he wanted to know if my mother cleans my room is because he said if she did then we'd have to pick a different place because maybe there'd be an accident. I didn't know what he was talking about."

"A different place for what? What's he doing? He's not stealing from you?"

He breathes out. "Nothing. He didn't do anything. He drove us to the beach today."

"Why didn't you call me?"

"I *always* call you!" His voice is low, sharp.

"Okay. Sorry. I thought you were with your father, that's all—"

"At home after the beach Paul saw me changing. He watched me."

My stomach twists like a dishcloth being wrung out. "Sean, *what*?"

His face is down. Maybe he's looking at the shells in the driveway, or maybe his eyes are closed. I can't tell. "I told him to go away, but he didn't. I was in the middle of changing. I was naked. And he said, 'I wanted to see your insulin pod. Wow, you're white down there,' he said in a weird voice, like whispering. He kept looking at me, even when I turned my back. I told him to get out. 'Come on,' he said. 'I have a brother. It's how you grow up.'"

"*What's* how you grow up?" I ask. "What's with him and growing up? Is he trying to be your dad?"

Sean's voice is nearly not there. "He touched me. I had nothing on. He made me do it. I almost threw up right on the floor."

"What are you talking about? Made you do what?" I'm shaking now. "My God, Sean, you have to tell. I'm telling!"

Sean grabs my arm tight, stares right into my face for what seems like minutes. Then he suddenly breaks into a laugh. But it's a high laugh, hoarse and shrill, not the way anyone really laughs. There's a sharp edge to it. "Got you!" he says. "Ha!"

"What?"

"I'm joking! Just to see if you'd believe me. And you did. You did!"

"Are you serious, this is all a joke?" I nearly cry from relief, but I'm angry. "Sean, you're such a jerk! What if I told somebody? I could have. I actually almost did." I feel heavy weights sliding off my back, even as my blood pumps like crazy.

"Got you, Owen Todd. Got you!"

I almost want to punch him, but what I do is growl. "You're such an idiot! I was so ready to tell. You mean everything's okay at home? He didn't do any of this?"

Sean lets go of my arm and starts bouncing on his toes, nodding.

"That's what you're saying, right? Powwl Landisss is okay after all? You made it all up? You made it up. The naked picture. All of it? You invented it?"

He laughs to himself and does a little tap dance on the shells, kicking them around with his toes. It's dark now, and the yards across the street are blackening.

"My dad will drive you home," I say.

"Nah." The way he says it reminds me of Paul Landis when I met him, just like his dance does. "Nah," he repeats and creeps back along the garage and around to the patio, peering at the window, where no one is standing now. "I can make it."

My heart is still hammering. "It's pretty dark."

He shrugs and heads backward across the patio to the hedge he came through. "Seriously, O, what's the worst that can happen?"

Chuckling so softly that I almost can't hear him, he fumbles through the bushes for an opening and is gone.

TEN

Got you. Ha!

Except it's not that easy. Sean's stung me, jerked me around, and I'm mad. As I stand on the dark patio, quivering, I run the whole thing over from the beginning and try to file it away, but something stinks like an old fish. You know what a fish story is. A story that gets more unbelievable each time you tell it. Like this:

Sean: "I caught a big fish today. It's ten pounds."

Owen: "That's not so big."

Sean: "You didn't let me finish. It's ten pounds on each side. It's twenty pounds, altogether."

Owen: "Twenty pounds still isn't that big."

Sean: "I mean just the head. If you count the tail, it's thirty pounds."

Owen: "It's thirty pounds now?"

Sean: "If you don't include the fins. They're forty pounds each."

Owen: "How many fins does it have?"

Sean: "How high can you count?"

So, is this what he did? I don't even know. I don't know whether to believe him or not. Why would he lie? And which part is a lie? That his babysitter tried this stuff, or that he didn't do anything except annoy Sean because Sean's got to have a babysitter and he's eleven? Either my best friend in the world has suddenly played a nasty trick on me—and on Paul—or it really *is* happening, and Sean can't tell me straight because it's too gross. *He touched me. I had nothing on.*

Either way, I feel dirty.

The next morning, I wake up twisted in my sheets and sweating, and I jump into the shower first thing. I'm finally ready to tell my parents or at least my dad what Sean told me, and let him decide what's real and what's a lie.

Until I'm walking downstairs to the kitchen and I hit the dining room.

The house around me looks so normal in the morning sunlight. The furniture, the wallpaper, the dust standing in the window light. I stop and look out at the driveway where we stood last night. It's just a driveway. I smell bacon, toast. I hear Ginny gurgling her juice and Mom laughing. I stop and stop and stop.

There's nothing to tell. Practically nothing.

The sentences I practiced in my mind fall apart in the light. Not only is it a gross thing to put words to, and grosser if it turns out to be wrong, I wouldn't get to hang with Sean anymore if it turns out he's lying and I repeat his lie. And what will my mom ever think of me, saying the words I'll have to say? Naked peeing? Nude pictures? Touching boys?

My chest buzzes just thinking about the expression on her face, in her eyes.

Then, when I step into the kitchen, Ginny's there at the table, red nosed and sniffling, my mom's hand on her forehead, whispering, "Better today, a little."

So . . . no. There's nothing to tell.

Better just take the sting of Sean's joke, accept that he fooled me, forget it, and move on with being normal.

As I sit down in my seat, Ginny twists a tissue into one nostril and lets it dangle there. "I'm sigg," she says, meaning "sick," and lets out a breath from her mouth that puffs the tissue up in front of her face.

"Don't breathe on me," I tell her.

"But I'm sigg!"

The laugh I laugh sounds a little stiff coming from my

mouth. Hoping it doesn't show, I wiggle a strip of bacon from my teeth and say, "Oh, wait. I'm sigg, too!"

Ginny and I laugh together.

I don't tell Mom or Dad about Sean. It's a story only for me. It's in the past. It's nothing. A practical joke. A strange one, maybe, but it's because he's angry he has to have a sitter. I finish eating, then bounce up from the table, rinse my plate in the sink, see the patio, and think about Sean last night.

"You know what, I think I'll go see what Austin's up to."

"Oh?" Dad looks up at me. "What about the side garden? You were going to clean that out and put the wood chips down."

"Oh, yeah. I will."

"Everything okay?" says Mom. "Isn't Sean back yet?"

"Yeah. I guess. I don't know. I've just sort of . . . Sean's okay. It's just we have another game coming up. Austin and I can toss the ball around. I'll show him a thing or two. We'll win. For the first time ever." It's lame, clunky, but I think it's enough, and I casually leave the kitchen.

Ginny trots after me, passes me at the bottom of the stairs, and crawls up on her hands and knees. She lifts her arms jerkily, like a marionette, and groans at each step, "I'm a bubbet. A sigg bubbet!"

"You're goofy, I know that much."

Ginny makes a face. "I'm going back to sleep."

Then I hear my parents talking low. ". . . have any *problem*," my father says, exaggerating the word as if the idea is silly. "Even friends have glitches, if that's what you mean."

Ginny reaches the top step, lies down on the landing.

"I mean . . ." Mom is saying, but I don't hear what she means because she says it softly and Ginny is still groaning. I step down a few stairs and listen.

"He's okay." My dad squeaks his chair away from the table. The coffeepot clinks. "I would know."

Finally, I tiptoe back up the stairs, all coiled around inside. When I pass the bathroom I see Ginny on the pot with her head down, humming. I close the door on her. She keeps humming. I go to my room for nothing, stand in the middle of the floor. I decide to myself that I'll skip the game tomorrow, so I won't see Sean. Maybe I'll do something, pretend I hurt myself pulling a muscle weeding the overgrown garden. Something like that, so I won't have to play. I need time away from him. I trot back downstairs through the kitchen with a smile.

"You know what? I'll do the yard work instead. All of it." I head to the back door.

"Wait," Mom says.

"Mom, I'm fine—" I start, but that's not it.

"I'm thinking of going to the beach after your game

tomorrow," she says, reaching for her cell phone, which is on the table, then unreaching. "Wellfleet."

I know the place. It's an out-of-the-way beach we've been to a few times, but not recently. It's nice. Quiet. But I don't want to play baseball, don't want to see Sean. Then, an idea.

"Ginny, too?" I ask. "Just us?"

"She has ballet," my dad says. "Or she might need to stay home with her cold. Either way, Uncle Jimmy will handle the track. I already asked him."

Then Mom spins around, her phone in her hand. "I thought we'd invite Sean."

"What? Mom, I don't—"

"Just you and Shay," she says, and before I know it she's tapped Mrs. Huff's number and is waiting for her to pick up. "He needs a break from his sitter. You, me, Sean, the beach. It'll be good."

I'm spinning. Not really, no. It won't be good. I don't want to see Sean.

ELEVEN

So that day, Friday, I stick around to do the yard like I promised. It turns out to be a beautiful morning. Seventy-three degrees, sunny, big-skied. My dad leaves for the track. Ginny finally goes back to bed. Later, while I'm dragging some bags of wood chips from the shed to the back border, Sean phones.

Mom answers, leans halfway out the screen door to the patio. "Owen, it's Sean about tomorrow!"

"I'll call him back. My hands are all dirty." I figure if he hears me yell this, he'll know I'm busy.

I don't call him back. He calls again in the afternoon. Mom shouts upstairs, but I make it obvious I'm getting in the shower and can't take the call. While I'm letting hot water drip over me, I decide it's lame to do something to get out of the game, like I'm the one playing tricks now, so I don't. But I don't call him back and don't see him all day. It's my way of getting even.

―――――――――

Dad drops me at the field Saturday morning. I delay as much as possible before we leave the house so it's practically game time when we get there.

"I wish I could stay," Dad says. "But I see Sean's already here. Mom'll come before the end of the game. I'm popping over to the track for a bit, then Ginny's staying home with me. Have fun at the beach."

"No problem." I watch him drive away. I see there's a beach bag tucked next to Sean's cooler under the first base bench. Coach is finishing a pep talk, but I can tell from his face he's really hoping Kyle will just miraculously float down from the treetops, swinging a bat and smiling like he always does.

But no. Kyle's not floating in, and we're going to lose worse than ever.

I apologize to Coach for being late, hustle out to center field, and the game begins. Good. No bench time with Sean.

The game, however, this game I wanted so much to miss, is finally a surprise.

The team from Orleans is smart and together and they score a run in each of the first three innings, once with a man on base. It's 4–0. In the fourth, John Pelosic hits a lone double for us and then incredibly steals it into a run. Who knew John could sprint that fast? 4–1. I'm waiting in center, but all the Orleans hits are going right. Without Kyle, our own hitting is nonexistent. Back and forth, on the field or waiting to bat, I don't say a word to Sean, though every time I catch a glimpse of him, he's staring at me like he wants to talk. I look away and mingle with the other players.

Despite his small size, the Orleans catcher is a power hitter, and the big excitement of the fifth inning is when he blasts a line drive past both Austin, who's pitching, and Adam, our second baseman. As soon as I hear the crack of the bat, I run in a little. The ball shoots past second, and I'm prepared to go either right or left if it bounces. The runner's nearly at first. The ball comes to ground just outside the dirt and bounces left. I turn, glove it in the air, sweep it into my fingers, and shoot it to second, where Adam is waiting. The runner is between the bags. He slows when the ball slaps Adam's glove. Adam chases him back to first, tosses the ball to Eric Cimino who has a foot on the bag, but Eric chops at the toss and bungles it. It drops into the dirt. Now the runner spins back and slides into second before Eric can snatch up the ball. We all scream. Adam and I did our parts, but another run is set up to score.

That happens two batters later with an into-the-trees home run, so both the hitter and the guy on second trot home easily. Score: 6–1.

Then, in the sixth inning, with the score 7–1, something big happens.

The sun has dried the morning dew, and in center the freshly mowed grass is just soaking up the heat. I glance over at Sean. He's looking small in his shallow spot in left, and I want to feel angry, but I'm not really mad. I don't know why. Maybe it comes to me that after everything, he's been my friend too long to keep this dark thing going. The anger's been grinding at me, and it's not worth it. I glance up, the sun is beaming overhead like God looking down, and I find my bad feeling drying up like dew and vanishing into air.

I'm still planted on the grass, legs apart, but somehow lighter. I look over at Sean again. Maybe sensing me, he turns and mouths something. I don't make it out because suddenly there's a sharp crack.

It's a power drive just inside the third-base bag, a low fast arc to Sean. This is actually pretty rare. As Coach has told us a hundred times, Little League batters hit mostly to right field and even if they hit to left, the hits are low and weak, so the fielder usually just chases down the ball and tosses it to second or third, a short throw.

Well, Sean's not ready. The ball smacks the grass about ten feet in front of him. I run toward it for back-up, but he's way closer and he finally hustles to grab it, except it bounces askew and he skids on the grass into a sitting position, with the ball having bobbled up off the ground and into his glove. I think he's surprised he actually has it, because he looks around first before seeing it in his glove.

"Sean! Sean!" Adam screams at second, grasping at the air for the ball that Sean hasn't thrown yet. But with the runner chugging toward Adam, it's already too late to throw to him.

"Sean, to third!" I yell. He could stop the runner there, but he doesn't. He takes the ball from his glove and lobs a slow one somewhere beyond second, almost to me. It comes down halfway between second and third like a brick out of heaven. *Plop.* No one is there.

You understand that all this takes no more than a few seconds.

"Sean, you ass!" someone yells.

I run to the ball along with everyone else now. Adam from second, Austin from the mound, Danny Zabin at third, everyone.

Suddenly, I hear my mom's voice out of the stands— "Go, Sean!" she's cheering, "Go, Sean!"—and he's the only one who isn't doing anything, I guess because he's thinking it would be dumb if he actually fielded the ball he threw.

With everyone converging on that tiny spot between second and third, the runner jerks sideways, stupefied, as if a rope tying him to second has suddenly grown taut. Then he resets and powers toward third, jumping over the rolling ball and weaving through the traffic jam.

"Hey, idiot! You idiot!" people shout. At Sean? At me? I don't know, but I find I'm running at a crouch, sliding my glove along the ground, and—*thwip!*—I feel the ball's weight. I whip it into my fingers, reaching back to throw.

Then something tells me to wait. Just wait. Wait long enough for the runner to tag third and roar to the plate. He does. I bullet the ball home, hoping the catcher will just do his job and get the guy out. The ball seems to hang in space for an hour or two before—*slap*—it's in the catcher's mitt, and the runner's out.

Coach's head, arms, legs explode. He screams at the top of his lungs like a lunatic. "You kids! I knew it! I knew it!" Half the team is standing in the red dirt between second and third, even Sean's there now, checking his upper arm under his sleeve. There's a moment when we're all jumping as if we won the game.

We don't, of course. Our moment of glory is all reversed in the top of the last inning. There are two outs. I'm at bat, and Sean's on deck.

"I want to hit," he says to me. "Don't you dare strike out."

I can't tell whether he's serious or joking until he says, "Please? Please, please!"

I snort. "Oh, dude, I got this." I even point my bat out to right field as if that's where I'm going to hit to. "I got this."

"You better."

"I do."

"You better do."

The pitches come startlingly fast. Before I know it, it's one ball, two strikes. I wait for a good one. No pressure swings, I say to myself, just wait for the right pitch. The first is outside. Ball two. The next pitch overcompensates and nearly smacks my hip. Ball three. I back away, look up at the blue sky. It's all so perfect. I take three, four practice swings.

"Come on," the catcher snarls under his breath. "Strike out, already."

I step back into the batter's box.

I crouch for the pitch.

I strike out.

I hear Sean groan for a half second before the Orleans

team sends up a huge shout, and the game is over, 8–1. I blow it, but that magical play is still in my head. My rocket ball to home plate is classic. Sean trots to the bench, stops, waits for me.

"We did it," he says. "Some play. I throw to you, you throw to home? Out!"

I didn't see it that way, of course. It *wasn't* that way. Sean totally bobbled the ball. But I let it go. Coach is still in heaven, grinning ear to ear, animated. Mom is dancing down from the stands, smiling, hugging me, jangling her keys. Sean grabs his cooler and beach bag. I'm swept into it.

TWELVE

So, Wellfleet.

It's halfway up the forearm, nearing the skinny wrist below P-town. I've been a handful of times, not lately, and Sean, never. The east side of the highway going up the Cape is mostly the National Seashore, so to get to the town beach, you take a left, drive up and down and into the center of town, which isn't big, and is sort of laid back, a little frayed, "shabby, even," Mom says, "but Wellfleet is where the famous oysters come from."

"What famous oysters?" Shay asks.

"Wellfleet oysters," I say.

He snorts. "That makes sense."

We wind through the streets, cross a couple of skinny roads through marshes, and head up a hill and then over to the beach, which Mom tells us is called "the Gut."

"It's where those famous oysters end up," Sean says.

"Ha." Mom slows the car. "Here we are."

She parks at the top of a road leading to the beach. We grab our stuff and work down to the bottom of the road, which ends in sand. Even with arms loaded, I scramble up an overgrown sandy path between a pair of narrow-slatted fences.

From the crest you can see the giant bowl of Cape Cod Bay. The shore below stretches wide and long beneath high cliffs of sand and goes deep out into the blue water. The surface is clean and calm. Straight west across the bay is Plymouth, where the Pilgrims landed. There's a stiff breeze coming over the crest. I lean into it. A second later my back tingles. I feel Sean move up behind me and linger there. I don't turn to him, just look at the bay.

———————

I want to say the ride out here was normal. It wasn't. I talked. Mom did. Sean talked. He told us about his mother's job, her rough first few weeks there, the summer movies he wanted to see, how his mother had to order a new batch of pods, because the last bunch had some that didn't work, and now he's wearing his second-to-last one, and maybe we didn't see but he fell on it during the game, though it's working fine.

It all seemed regular, but despite not being angry anymore, I'm keeping a part of myself back. I'm not completely me, not like you're yourself and you know you are and it's just you. No. I'm a little off. Words are collecting in my throat but they won't come out. I don't think my mom noticed while we were in the car. She was busy driving, but maybe she did.

One thing.

When we drove left off Route 6 at the Wellfleet sign, Sean shifted next to me to get into his beach bag—we're side by side in the back seat—and his elbow slid across my forearm. Without thinking, I flinched as if I'd been stuck by a pin or shocked by static.

"What the heck?" he said. "You could move."

And it's suddenly different. As if even my arm knows that something's not right, something has changed. His touch tingled on my skin and my stomach felt it, and I remembered Paul in his room when he was changing. I felt bad to think that way, to act like that, but there you are.

Mom asked about his fall on the field.

"I'm fine," he said.

After that, we mostly just looked out our open windows.

Right now, as I'm standing on the crest of the dune, him behind me, I still feel what it felt like when his arm brushed mine. At any minute, Sean could blow it all with another story—real or not, it doesn't matter. I can't seem to move. I hold my breath. I actually feel my blood running in my veins.

I try to shake off the feeling, and scan the beach.

To our left is a curving taper of sandbar in the shape of Mexico. There are a couple of families there, maybe more, with little kids scouring the wet sand for shells.

Sean looks out over it too. "Nice." I turn finally. He rests a beach chair against his leg. His hair flips up in the breeze, then settles. He runs a hand through it.

"It's pretty quiet here," I say. "That's probably the best thing about it. You forget everything going on back there." I tilt my head to mean Brewster. I realize I did that for myself. I want to get away from what's going on there as much as he does.

"Smell that?" I ask.

"Perfumey."

"Beach roses," I tell him.

"Oh. Right."

All along the crest of the dune among the long grasses are thickets of prickly stemmed wild roses—my mother calls them "beach roses," though not everyone does, and I'm not sure if there are actually two different kinds of roses, beach and wild. Most of the blooms near us are pink, with white ones here and there.

The papery petals smell different than regular roses do. An open beach rose is an amazing thing. It's rained on, blown on, sunned on, and all the while gives out its scent. By the end of the summer the petals will have flown away and turned brown and disappeared into the grasses and down along the path to the cars.

"Have you ever sniffed both colors to see if there's a difference?" I ask stupidly, but he doesn't answer anyway. "I think pink are a little sweeter." I lean over to one, then the other. "I like the white ones—"

"There's probably no difference." He looks at the water. "Come on. There's not a lot of time."

"We have the rest of the day," I say, but he steps past me down the steep dune toward the flatness of the sand. A red umbrella flashes open to my right, and a girl laughs. I feel cold in the sunshine. My blood runs chilly, and my neck hurts.

"Are you coming?" he asks, half turning his head.

Is he going to wreck it for me?

I try to remember standing in the grass at center field just this morning, try to remember how light I felt and how calm. But just like on the field, I feel that the peace here could be broken so easily. Stealing a glance back at my mother, beach umbrella tucked under her arm, lugging a bulging beach bag, I want to run back to help, but she smiles and says, "Go on!" and Sean's still looking at me. So I take a breath and follow him over the crest and down to the sand.

At the bottom of the dune you can look right and left on this long inward curve of beach and you feel right at the handle of a bow. I think the tide is coming in, but the flatness goes out a long way, a calm white sheet.

Sean suddenly takes off, kicking the sand in front of him as he approaches the water, then dragging his feet. Is he playing or angry?

"Owen?" my mother calls from the crest. She nods to her left. "Let's set up over there." There are only a few people, three or four towels, and some giggling girls fooling with a Frisbee. It'll be quieter. Mom loves the quiet.

"Sean!" I call. He half turns, his hair flying in the breeze off the water. He's smiling, which surprises me. I tilt my head to the left. "Yonder!"

He spins twice around on his heels and slogs happily through the sand like it's snowdrifts. I think I can breathe again.

We dump our stuff: towels, his snack cooler, beach bags, folding chairs, baseball caps. We pop off our sneakers and trot back to help my mother with the last of the gear. In minutes, we're set up.

"Let's walk," I say.

"Honey, you need lotion, both of you do," Mom says. "Sean, do you need to eat? It's half past twelve."

"When we come back from our tour."

"Fifteen minutes. I'll time you."

We circle the sandbar, not talking for a bit. The sand is littered with shells. The tide is definitely coming in and there's less sandbar now than I saw from the top of the dune.

"Those guys charge so much," he says out of nowhere.

"What guys?"

"The crushed-shell people. They come down here and collect shells for free and stomp on them and put them in bags and sell them to you. What a scam."

"It's probably more complicated." I picture him standing alongside my garage, staring out to my driveway. I try to think of anything else than how he tricked me, but I can't. I want to say something, but it would be so tense. I don't.

Sean grins "Did I tell you—" Suddenly a red blade slices his face.

"Ahhh!" he screams, clutching his nose. Then he looks at his hands. Nothing. His nose is fine. "What the—" A Frisbee is lying in the sand at his feet.

"Sorry!" a little girl shouts, running to us.

"She's sorry!" her friend says, also running. "OMG. *So* sorry!"

They must be six or seven and sparkling with sand, one with crazy red hair, the other with wet brown hair tied in a messy ponytail.

I snatch up the Frisbee. "This is a lethal weapon." They freeze in their tracks as if they think I'm serious or they don't know what the words mean. I make it worse. "You could have killed him." They look back at their blanket, but it's empty; their mothers or whoever are down at the water, dipping their toes in.

No help from them.

One girl's face goes as red as her hair. "But we're sorry."

"It's okay," Sean says with a laugh. He takes the Frisbee from me and bops it lightly on the ponytail girl's head.

She laughs nervously, steps back, puts her hands on her hips. "Want to play with us?"

Her friend slaps her arm. "No!"

I shake my head. "No, thanks." But Sean turns bizarre.

"We better not. My friend here is just out of jail and can't be with people just now. Jail's why he knows what a weapon is."

They both step back as if tied together.

"What? Liar!" I say.

Ponytail girl turns. "You boys are creepy. Both of you." They each jump back a few more steps and plop down on the sand, staring at us.

"We want our Frisbee back," says red hair. "Or we'll tell."

"Just a sec!" Sean runs backward, curling his arm around the Frisbee. "Owen, go out long. Let's replay the play we did on the field this morning!"

I laugh inside, since "going out long" is football, but I spring back anyway and splash along the water line up to my ankles, looking over my shoulder. He slings the disk. It's fast but low and dropping. "I got it!" I dive, right arm out, fingers reaching, and I clutch it, rolling over on my back in the sand and onto someone's beach blanket and into some plastic bottles. "Ow! Ow!"

But I quickly jump up, holding the Frisbee high. "Did you see that? Did you see that? Let's go to the video!"

The girls are screaming, but also laughing, I think, and Sean is laughing, too. "You have mustard on your butt!" he yells at me, and the girls scream louder when they hear the word. I toss them their Frisbee. They run away while Sean jumps around waving his arms. Is he okay again? I love it. He's back and he's normal.

"Hey!" Some middle-aged guy in red trunks that are too small for him hustles over to the blanket I trampled.

"Uh-oh," I say.

Sean stops jumping and watches the man with red trunks reach his blanket, shake his head at what he finds, then flop onto it. Something crashes in Sean, I don't know what. "I have to eat something." He says this quietly.

"I have some mustard on my butt. You could . . ." I don't go anywhere with that because it's gross. I try to laugh, but I can't.

"I have to eat," Sean says again as if he didn't hear me, which he did.

I don't know exactly what just happened, but something buzzes in my chest.

———————

Mom is reclining under the umbrella. It's a big one and Sean fits neatly under it, while I decide to sit on the open blanket. Mom didn't see our episode with the Frisbee or my fall on some guy's mustard, so I don't get the third degree.

"Lotion up," she says. "Everybody."

I do. I can take the sun pretty well, but I've gotten burns before that I don't want to repeat. Sean will probably stay under the umbrella. He burns easily. I put on my J&D Karts cap, slop some lotion on my shoulders, and sit, hugging my knees on the blanket in the sun. Sean opens his beach bag, takes out his test kit, pricks his finger, tests his blood, presses a button on his controller unit, and eats.

"Do you feel the insulin going in?" my mom asks.

"Nah. It's all timed out."

I pricked myself once and did a reading, but his mother got mad because my number screwed up the download of his numbers. Anyway, I'm not hungry now, so I just sit. Mom opens a book but doesn't read it. Instead she gets up and takes a plastic pail from her big bag. "Shells," she says, and goes by herself to the disappearing sandbar.

"What do people do with them anyway?" Sean asks after she leaves. "I mean, I know what driveway guys do and what your mom does, but everyone else who collects shells at the beach. Don't you just end up throwing them away?"

"I don't know."

My mom makes shell lamps. In fact, she's making a few for Mrs. Huff, who'll display them at her shop as a sideline. Shell lamps have clear glass bases that you fill with shells or beach glass and some sand. Mom has made some for us and sells others on consignment, which means she gets paid only when they actually sell. They're priced a few dollars more than an empty lamp, but they're so beachy that people like them.

"It's not a scam," I say. "To make beach lamps. There's the labor and the price of the lamp, so, you know . . ."

"I know. I wasn't saying that." He's getting quieter under the shadow of the umbrella.

Time passes. The beach is crowding up a little more now that it's afternoon and the tide is pressing in. More people bound past our setup, some with little on, teenage girls' thin shirts darkened by the shapes of the suits underneath, boys' chests bare and baggy shorts worn low. One girl with long black hair walks slowly by about ten feet away from our blanket.

"*She* should be your sitter," I whisper. "Man!"

"Listen," he says.

"In fact, I'm going to ask her. Wait here." I pretend to start to get up when he jerks up to a crouch.

"Listen, I . . ."

But Mom is back, one hand holding her pail full of shells, the other cradling her cell phone to her ear. "Linda," she says, setting the pail next to her beach chair and moving off again. "Yes? All right. Tuesday? Wonderful . . ."

Sean's looking down at the sand. He pulls his cap low and huddles under the umbrella like his stomach is convulsing.

I don't want to say it, but I do. "Sean, what are you trying to tell me?"

He screws up his face, his eyes shifting across the blanket in front of him. "It happened again," he says. "It happened again, only this time he did more . . ."

"Are you back on that? Seriously?" I cut him off. I don't

want to hear it. "You said you were joking. That was the end of it, you had your fun, now cut it out."

"I'm not joking. I wasn't joking." He says this softly, without emotion.

I feel my chest burn. "Really? Except what if you're joking now?" I get to my knees. "Let's just swim or something." Then I find myself saying what I almost told my mom when she announced he was coming with us. "You're lucky I still hang with you."

He ignores that, or maybe he doesn't. His face changes. His eyes burrow into the sand, and he grips his knees, closes them like a vise. "Paul said I'll like it. He said I'll feel good and make him feel good too." Now he opens and shuts his legs like a bellows.

"You can't do this," I hiss at him. I get up to my feet. "You can't tell me it's true if it isn't. Are you saying he hurt you? Come on, Sean, make up your mind!"

"I don't know. No. It doesn't hurt."

I'm down again. Hearing my mom's ringtone, I peek around the umbrella. She's kicking through the sand some way down the beach, still on the phone. "You have to tell your mom," I whisper. "This is too gross."

"I will. I will, but you can't."

"What *more* did he do?"

"I'm not telling you."

I don't know what to say. The tide has washed over the sandbar. Checking, I see my mother is off her phone now, and soon she is back with us. I clam up.

"That's two things next week," she says. "The newspaper might have a job for me, part-time to start, and Grandma is coming for a few days, too."

I nod mechanically. "You wanted to go back to work there. Good. Ginny should be done with her cold when Grandma comes."

"Oh, I hope so!" Mom says. "I'm sure." She sits on the blanket outside the umbrella, smiling as she empties the pail and arranges her shells in sizes and colors.

"Reapply, please," she says.

Sean is staring now. I feel his eyes on me. I know I'm not supposed to give any hint of what he just told me. I also know my mom is out of this completely, counting out her shells on the blanket. Am I supposed to fix this all by myself?

I need to think. I stand in the sun and put on another coat of lotion. Reapply. Reapply. We've done this for years. But today is different.

He said I'll feel good and make him feel good too. My stomach turns. *He did more.*

"I'm going in the water." I mean by myself. I step away down the sand.

"Just be where I can see you both," Mom says, ignorant that I want to be alone. "Sean, take it easy with your pod. Are you sure it won't come off?"

"It's okay. It's waterproof. But there's always the other one, if I need it." He opens his beach bag. "See?" His hands are shaking.

Without looking back, I run down the sand as if I don't care about anything. I wade in for a long way before I get to my waist. Splashing my chest and arms, I feel like the water, warm in July, is washing Sean's words off me. It feels good. As if I'm just me again. I wash him off. I dive under to get my face clean of the looks he gives me, to get his words and jokes out of my ears. I look out across the bay, away from the beach. The breeze rolls over me.

Finally, I turn.

Sean hasn't left the blanket. He's pretending to look around like everything's fine. What a faker. Maybe he's talking with my mother. I don't know. Her eyes are closed and she's half in, half out of the umbrella's shade. I watch him glance over at her, then stand up slowly. He checks the seal on his pod and he runs to the water. He sloshes in, keeping his pod arm under the water, and I wonder if it really will stay on. I don't move. I don't want to talk to him.

But he doesn't come to me.

He swims out away from me, both little white arms slapping the surface, his head turning this way and that like a real swimmer. I worry again about his pod. I want to yell to him about it. I don't.

I go out only as far as I can feel the bottom a few inches under me, bouncing up and down on my toes to keep my neck and head out of the water.

Sean is in beyond his height, my height, too. A tingle runs through my chest. He bobs, keeping afloat by pushing the water down with his palms. It's deep.

"Sean!" I call.

He stops.

He stops moving his arms. He goes completely still. His face is a small sad circle of eyes and nose and white lips, his hair short, wet, dark. I realize at that moment how far away from me he is.

Without gulping air, without making it seem like he's diving, because he isn't, Sean sinks.

"Hey," I yell at him, knowing his ears are filled with water. I edge out beyond my limit, bouncing high from the bottom and working my arms and hands to keep afloat. It gets colder the deeper I go. "Hey! Sean!"

I wait for him to come back up, but he doesn't.

He doesn't come up. My blood runs colder than the chilly water. I swish around. We are far out, and the tide is still coming in. Turning for a half second, I can't spot my mother right away. "Mom!" I scream.

There is a splash.

Sean's head breaks the surface, his face a white ghost, his eyes open, his hair streaming over his forehead. I want to punch him.

"What the heck are you doing?" This is not what I really say. I curse him. Then I scream, "What are you doing?"

He sloshes noisily toward me, past me, sloppily past me. "Nothing."

He's back where he can touch the bottom. He's walking now, but his pod is hanging off; the sticky seal has broken.

"You need . . ." I start, but don't finish. I follow him back in. I'm exhausted by the time we make it to the sand. He drags the water heavily with him up the slope of the beach, then he stops.

We're still out of hearing of my mother, of everyone.

"Look, I don't care if you believe me," he says, looking at the sand between his feet. "Paul made me do things. I can't tell you what. I won't ever tell you."

I swallow the lump in my throat. "He touched you? Down there? Is that what you're saying? What *are* you saying?"

"He touched me and I touched him."

"That's so sick. Shay, you did not."

"He said it was okay that we touch. And *touched* isn't even what he was doing, what his fingers were doing. He

110

said he's moving away at the end of the summer anyway, leaving the Cape, so it's just for a little while. You have to promise me that you won't ever tell."

Sean sounds as if he's sobbing, but he isn't. Not on the outside. Not in his eyes.

"No. I won't do that."

"Promise me, Owen. Because if you tell somebody—*anybody*—I'll kill myself. I know how. I totally know how and I can."

The words knife me in the throat. *I'll kill myself.* Kids our age never do that. Only high school kids do that when they're bullied. And that's one every five years, right?

Or maybe I don't know anything about it.

There is a look in his eyes. Even in that bright sunlight, his eyes are dark, as if all the white has drained out of them and only black irises remain. His glare swallows me and everything else around us—the color, the running children, the girls in bikinis, the families, their movements. The whole place except him just dies. He's quivering. His outline blurs as if he's dizzy and going to faint, or I am. I can't even tell. The white sand turns black around us. I'm afraid for him. And for me. I close my eyes so I don't fall over, so I don't have to look at his face.

"It's just for a little while. Owen, promise me. I'll get over it. I will." Then, water beading his cheeks and his quivering chin, he says very slowly through his teeth: "You have to promise, or I will be dead!"

"Stop saying that!"

In a whisper: "If you tell, I will *kill* myself!"

The *k* cuts again, cuts into me this time. And I suddenly remember that his father works with guns. Is there a gun at his house? My insides become water, and they want to empty out of me right on the beach. I tighten the muscles in my rear to keep it from happening. I say the words.

"All right."

"All right what?" He steps closer to me, breathes his sweet bad breath on my face. "Owen, all right *what*?"

"All right. I promise."

"Say it. The whole thing."

"I promise not to tell."

"You promise not to tell anyone ever."

"I promise not to tell anyone ever."

THIRTEEN

The rest of the afternoon, my mind is a tangled mess.
After Sean gets to the umbrella, he peels off his old pod
and switches to the new one in his bag. He says it doesn't
hurt, but he winces when he clicks the inserter under his
skin.

"Good for another three days," he says, then lies about
how he loves the water, the sun, all that, and finally sits
there like a lump. Mom soon falls asleep over her book,
so it doesn't matter that we turn dead silent.

I feel as heavy as stone. After a while, I leave him there
and walk and walk and walk along the shore, kicking at
the incoming waves. The Frisbee girls are at it again. I
avoid them and everybody else. A couple of teenagers are
snuggled near the cliff, making out and all over each other.
It takes me a minute to realize they're two boys.

I turn away, go back, turn again and keep going. The tide is starting to go out. How long have I been walking?

When I get back, my mother's awake. Most of our things are stowed.

"We're going?"

"Sean's not feeling well," she says. "But he didn't want me to call you back to the blanket."

I'll bet he didn't.

"It's okay," I say, still not looking at Sean, but trying to smile for my mother. "We can go."

As we collect the last bits, Mom asks Sean if we need to call his mother, and when he shrugs, she calls anyway. "She'll meet us at your house."

In the car, I barely look at him, terrified that if I say anything at all, or my mother says something, he'll bring on his I-want-to-die face again. We aren't talking. The words in my throat have turned to lead.

When we get back on Route 6, my mother looks in the rearview. "So, great beach, isn't it? What a day." Mumbled responses from Sean and me. "Again, I'm sorry you don't feel well, Sean. You guys all right? Did something happen?"

"No. It was awesome," Sean says. He sounds normal. He's a good faker. "I get a headache every once in a while. Mom gets them, too."

"I'm sorry, I know she does," Mom says, and I realize that Mrs. Huff is often frowning, like she's in pain. Maybe that part of Sean's problem is real. "We can come back sometime when you're feeling better. If you guys are up for it. You had fun, right?"

Sean nods at her in the rearview. "Sure. That'd be great."

I'm not so sure. But I don't say that or anything else, and just let it pass.

An hour later, we're back in Brewster. We drive to Sean's house. I hold my breath from the corner on, hoping I'll see Mrs. Huff's car in the drive. It isn't there. We pull up at the curb.

"Let me call your mom again." My mom slips her cell phone out of her bag.

His house isn't all that old and looks like a lot of the houses here. Wooden shingles that the rain and sun have beaten to a rough gray. It's small, but neat. Bright white window trim. Crushed shells in the short driveway. The house has a main section, an upstairs with dormers in front and back, and one room coming off the side of the downstairs that makes an L into the backyard. There are two rooms there, a bathroom and Sean's room. In the backyard there's a patio and a small in-ground pool that is empty and fenced off because it needs fixing.

"Your mom's stuck at the store until tonight," my mother says. "I told her we'll bring you home with us, but she's sure it'll be hours and already called Paul. I don't know why she does that. Not let us help. Anyway, he should be here soon." She turns off the engine. "She said just a few minutes."

Sean bites his lip. "Okay. Thanks."

I begin to realize that it's little things like this—snarled traffic, a phone call, rain, some new job, whatever it is—that make all the difference about whether things go good or bad. You tiptoe around stuff or you kick it away or you crush it, but whatever is going to happen happens anyway because of stuff you can't control.

"Thanks for the trip. I'll wait in the backyard." Sean tears across the lawn and around the back.

Mom turns to me. "Something's bothering Sean. Did you have a fight?"

"No, Mom. Of course not. He's just tired. He has a headache. It's okay." It looks bad for me to just sit in the car. I don't want to talk to Sean any more than I have to, but I can't talk to my mom like this, either. I remember the empty pool, I don't know why. "I guess I'll wait with him in the backyard."

Sean's yard is as trim as his house, with short flowers edging around a barrier of low, pointy evergreens. The neighbor who mows the lawn must have just been there. The smell of fresh-cut grass, like the smell of beach roses and sunny ball fields, is summer to me.

It's quiet back there except for a couple of mowers a block or two away. We just stand, staring at the ground.

"Sean, listen . . ." I don't know where I'm going with this, but I kind of blurt out, "Swimming all the way out like that—"

Suddenly, he crouches like a hunter. "Did you see it?" His arms tense as his eyes follow a small brown shape, skittering along the patio retaining wall and heading for the toolshed.

"What, the chipmunk?"

"It's a mouse," he says. "A big mouse. It's trying to get in the shed."

"No, it isn't. It's a chipmunk. It's Chip and Dale. Chip *or* Dale."

Sean scrabbles for a rock near the wall, finds one, and throws it. Fantastically, he manages to hit the animal just off the patio. The little thing hops once, then stumbles away into the garden.

"Sean, what the heck!"

My mother beeps. Disgusted, I leave Sean on the patio and come around to see Paul Landis pulling into the driveway. I look back. Sean edges after me slowly. Now I see someone else in the car. It's a girl. Paul's girlfriend is with him today. My chest zings. Good. Great!

"Hi," she says to us as she gets out. "I'm Carrie."

Carrie has a big, open smile. Does her being here mean she doesn't know anything about what her boyfriend does?

"Well, isn't this nice. Spur of the moment. Hi, Patti," Paul says to my mom. I'm surprised to hear him say her name, but of course they know each other from church.

She nods, smiling. "Really, we would have taken Sean home with us."

"Nah, I was close by." He bounces up the steps and unlocks the front door. He has a key, which I didn't know, but of course he would. He slips inside the house as if it's his own, letting the screen door flutter closed behind him.

Carrie comes over to us, shaking hands with my mother first before turning to me. Sean is hanging by the corner of the house. "Are you . . . you're Owen, right?"

"Uh-huh." I wonder if it was Sean or Paul who told her that, but I smile anyway, and she beams. She is cute. But it doesn't make any sense. If Paul has such a good-looking girlfriend, why does he need to do stuff like what Sean is telling me?

"All right, then," Mom says. "See you, Sean. Thanks for a nice day."

I look at him. His eyes are down as he walks slowly around and up the front steps with Carrie. She puts her hand on his shoulder like a teacher. He doesn't flinch. He might even lean toward her, but maybe not. She waves back at us. Maybe it will be okay with her there.

I glance at Sean's room on the side of the house. His

shade is up, the window blue with sky. I wonder what will happen. I hope Carrie stays the whole time. The front door closes behind them.

I feel like my face is completely draining of color and pray my mother doesn't see it or ask me anything. But she does see. She does ask. Instead of starting the car, she sits behind the wheel, looking at me.

"Owen, what is it?"

"Nothing. A chipmunk. In his backyard."

"Come on, O. That's not it. You've been quiet all day. Sean, too. You fought. Or something. What's going on with you two?"

"I . . ." But I don't know where I'm going with this. My mom is open and ready to listen, her brown-green eyes soft, almost moist, and looking at me so intently, wanting to put her hand on my arm or something, but not doing it. I have to glance away. Then I see Paul gazing out the picture window in the front of the house, his hands on his hips. He moves away, and I see that Carrie was standing behind him. She waves at our car.

"I think Sean sort of lied to me about something," I say. "I don't know. Maybe I'm wrong. I hope so."

Mom waves at Carrie. "What do you think he lied about?"

It's just for a little while, Sean said Paul told him. *A little while.*

119

"I don't know. I'll figure it out. It's okay."

She draws a breath in slowly, loudly. "All right. But you *can* talk to your mother, you know. I understand things. Your dad, too. He was a boy once."

"I know."

She starts the car. "You're thinking kids. You both are." She leans over, kisses me on the cheek. "I love you, you know."

I make a show of wiping my cheek. *Mom!* I want to scream. *Mom!* But the words I need to say jumble on my tongue and I swallow them. "Love you, too."

"Okay, then. Just so we both know that." She puts the car in gear. We drive the six short blocks home.

FOURTEEN

That was Saturday.

I think about Sean every day after that, but I don't call him. Now that I've made my ugly promise, he'll keep telling me stuff, because he probably has to. But unless he calls, I can believe things aren't getting any worse.

I don't actually talk to him until Wednesday, first thing in the morning, when he calls my house at breakfast.

"I'm off to visit my grandparents," he says. His voice is back to normal, no darkness in it, not yet.

"Oh, yeah?"

"They live in Quincy. I have to go, but I also want to. My mother's doing overnight inventory at the shop, top to bottom, for a couple of nights. Belle-Teak is in crisis mode."

"Again?"

"People are still stealing stuff."

"It looks pretty easy to," I say. "The racks outside, anybody can come along."

"No, that's cheap stuff. Scarves and things and cheap dresses. Mom suspects one of the sales girls, but whoever it is, is clever. There are three of them now. Two others besides the Goth girl. People suck."

I wonder how Mrs. Huff could be suspicious of her staff and not of Paul, but then, she's always worrying about one thing or another and often isn't *there* when you talk to her. "You could come here, I guess. You know, sleep over."

"I want to go to Quincy," he repeats. "Besides, it's my grandfather's birthday coming up in a couple of weeks. I begged to go. I haven't seen them for a while."

"Can you . . ." I stop. I won't ask. Then I remember. "My grandma's coming on Friday anyway."

"See ya."

He hangs up, and I feel free for a couple of days at least. I'll be more normal than if he was around, and if Paul Landis leaves town, the problem might actually go away. Sean said he'd get over it. Maybe he will. I wonder if I should ask Mom or Dad about whether they heard if Paul's moving, but that would open up a big thing that could be messy.

Anyway, good.

Sean and I won't see each other and he'll be safe with his grandparents.

I say that to myself. *Safe.* But I still don't know if it'll be true. Maybe I just mean that he'll be safe from himself. But I don't know that, either.

My dad wonders about rain coming later in the day, so he says I can stay home if I want to. I do stay home, but Mom wants to do some shopping at the mall before she starts her new two-day-a-week job, so she, Ginny, and I all go. I get a windbreaker. Ginny's cold is better.

It does end up raining after all, starting in late morning. Practice is canceled. Then, because Wednesday's lousy weather moves out at night, Dad predicts Thursday will boom at the track, so I go with him, and he's right. It's nonstop. I'm frantically spritzing seats all day long.

"We nearly made up for yesterday's loss," Dad says, flipping a stack of receipts.

"Nearly," Jimmy adds. "But is having a solid week of sun too much to ask?"

Grandma lives a little over an hour away in Hanover and is due at our house in the late morning, but getting to the Cape on a Friday in summer is a bad idea, especially if it's a nice day, and the morning is beautiful, so I'm not all that surprised when I come inside after trimming the lawn to find she hasn't gotten there and it's nearly noon.

What does surprise me is Ginny. For some reason she's dressed in green from head to ballet slippers and jumping up and down on the kitchen floor, yelling, "Pee! Pee! Pee! Pee!"

I laugh. "So go, already."

"Not without Grandma!"

This throws me. "You *are* toilet trained. I think I remember that."

"Not *pee*!" she says, then points to her green tights and green short shorts. "P . . . P . . . P . . . P!"

Which sounds the same to me. "Good luck with that."

"The play! I already told you!" She's shouting everything at the top of her lungs.

"No, you didn't. I wish people would stop not telling me things."

"Peter Pan Puppet Play," she spurts. "We're supposed to see it but Grandma's late and we need to get seats and Mommy's working and Daddy's going to the track. Daddy's always going to the track. Track, track, track!"

Then maybe I remember that Ginny did say something about puppets. I strain to put it together. There's a small outdoor children's theater in Dennis. It's tucked away in a patch of trees, all piney and woodsy.

I hear the clear crunch of shells through the open window.

"Here she is!" Ginny starts jumping again. "Grandma! P-P-P-P!" She runs out the door to the car.

"Thank God." My dad's rolling his eyes as he comes through the kitchen, jangling his keys, then pauses to look me up and down. "You going like that? In your yard clothes?"

"I forgot all about it."

"Your grandmother came to see you, too, you know."

"I'll change!" I turn to go upstairs when Grandma comes toddling in the door, saying, "Pee, pee, pee! That's what I have to do. Hello, Dale." She kisses my dad, then me, then runs to the bathroom. "Get in the car, kids. I know I'm late. Does anyone know the way?" I hear the squeak of the toilet seat.

"Just down the street, Grandma," I call. I run up and change my shirt, get into shorts, and am right back down. I hurry out, Grandma close behind. Ginny is a green elf in the car seat. She barely fits in it anymore. Dad locks up the house and a minute later drives off to the track with a wave. We are on the road to a puppet show.

Eighteen minutes later the three of us are trekking up a long path through scrubby woods into a kind of wild fairyland in the middle of a stand of old pine trees. I carry an enormous bag Grandma pulled from the trunk. The theater is smaller than I remember, even with a new proscenium arch around it. The stage is just planks mounted about a foot above the ground, and surrounded by five sets of risers in a shallow half circle. There's a lime green curtain hanging from the arch, and the stands are already pretty full. Grandma's nimble, but she's breathing hard by the time we climb to the back row of risers and take some of the last spots. She tucks her bag between her feet and slides out a small cushion that she puts on the riser under her before she plunks down.

"My butt pad," she whispers to me. "There. Ooof."

But Ginny is grumbling. "I can't see. We're late and I can't see. Why are grown-ups so big?"

"If this is like the original play," Grandma says, "Peter flies. You'll be at eye level!" She chuckles.

"Did you see the original play?" Ginny asks.

"A hundred years ago? Yes, dear."

"Wow."

Grandma leans over to me. "Thank goodness I made it in time. Traffic was, well, you know. I should have known."

"Ginny was ready to explode."

"That would have been messy."

Ginny still seems ready to blow up. She's squirming, crouching, stretching, bouncing, standing on tiptoes, plopping down again.

"Don't fidget, dear."

"But I can't see!"

"Because it hasn't started yet," I say, which doesn't help. Then I spot Kyle Mahon at the entrance. I wave. He's got his arm on his little brother's shoulder and is looking around. He doesn't see me. The stands are nearly full, but there are two places next to us. Their mother waits by a tree, chewing her lip.

The show is about to start. Actors—no, puppeteers— are moving backstage, flapping the curtain a little. It's hot. I wave again. Kyle sees this time. He nods and smiles, gives a thumbs-up. He nudges his brother—Eric? Spencer? Bruno? I have no idea—and they start climbing up the edge of the risers to the rear. Their mother steps back and leans against the tree trunk as if she'll stay there.

A thin boy pokes his head out from behind the curtain. He is dressed in black and wears black gloves. "If the little ones want to come down front, they can get an extra-special view. Anyone?"

Ginny gasps, and the horde of kids cheers and tumbles down from the stands just as Kyle and his brother ease their way along the back riser to us. Ginny is on her feet again, waving at Kyle's little brother. "Morgan! Let's go down front!"

Morgan—who knew?—yelps, and they teeter down the risers together and plop themselves into the soup of squirming toddlers. Grandma scooches over, and Kyle sits next to me, laughing.

"Ginny looks like one of the lost boys," he says and introduces himself to my grandmother as a classmate and a baseball friend.

"You a Pan fan?" I ask, having just come up with the rhyme.

"Yeah. I empathize because I can't grow up. Never gonna. Not me."

Grandma chuckles. "I wonder how they'll treat the Indians. There are Indians in the play, you know. They can't do it the way they used to. Too racist. Ha! As if you can be a little racist."

Kyle nods. "They changed the native people to sort of generic settlers, and their songs have changed. I read about it."

"Ah," she says, "I do like when settlers sing."

"How was your vacation?" I ask.

Kyle leans over to me. "They have no clue what a beach is down there. Dad was grumpy the whole time about work. I'm kind of glad to be back. Coach is, too. I heard about the game with Orleans. Nice play. Coach told me."

"He told you?"

"Yeah. Sounds like a real traffic jam at second, but you pulled it out. And waiting for the runner to dash for home? Excellent."

I'm about to respond when the curtain parts in the middle and swishes to the sides with a recorded fanfare of trumpets and flutes, except you can hardly hear them over the kids in front yelling and clapping.

We see the home of the Darling family in London, where there is a sudden rush of dangly puppets on strings, marionettes, worked from above the stage by black-shirted, black-gloved kids. A great window is open at the back of the room, and through it you can see the famous skyline of London painted on a backdrop.

Grandma is leaning over, almost rocking.

"Are you all right?" I whisper. "Grandma."

"I'm sorry, Owen. Is there . . . I need some water . . . and a quiet bench, maybe?"

"We passed some on the path," Kyle says across me. He points to the end of the row on Grandma's side. "It's shortest that way, and you can scoot around behind the risers."

It's all happening at once, the wobbly figures on stage, the marionettes laughing and screaming at Nana, the giant floppy dog that romps awkwardly from bed to bed, and now Grandma, standing and wobbling herself. I'm grateful that we're in the back row and not in front of anyone.

"A little less noise there!" Mr. Darling says to his spindly children and dangly dog. Of course, the audience shrieks, which sends Mr. Darling's arms flailing, so they shriek some more.

So many people in the row have to get up to let Grandma out. Then I realize of course that I have to go with her, so I follow, trying to stay clear of toes and keep my grandmother from toppling over. I hold her by the elbow, and it's so bony that something zings in my chest. Lullaby music is playing, and the Darling kids are in bed, and quiet, so people are looking at the two of us, clomping down the side of the stands to the ground.

I give a little wave to Ginny and stupidly show her a frown *and* a thumbs-up. I don't know what I mean by this, and neither does Ginny. Her mouth hangs open. She starts to get up, but I shake my head. Then Grandma and I move around the side of the risers to the back. We walk down the path to the parking lot, where there are two benches under the trees. Grandma is wheezing loudly and perspiring. I don't know what's wrong.

She plops down on the nearest bench, almost before she gets to it, then slides in from the edge. "Bring me some water, please."

I trot back to the ticket booth. "My grandmother isn't feeling well," I tell the girl, but she must have seen us already because she's digging behind the counter and snatching a water bottle for me.

"I have more if you need any. Do you want me to call anyone?" She's so nice.

"No. Thanks. Thank you."

"Just let me know." She can't be much younger than Paul Landis's girlfriend, and so nice, my throat tightens.

I hurry back to the bench. Grandma has her head low near her knees, but lifts her face. It's stark white, her forehead beaded with sweat. She takes the bottle. It's wet and her fingers slip. I grab it before it hits the ground. "Grandma, should I call Mom?"

She shakes her head as she drinks. I don't know what to do, so I sit next to her. She's warm. She drinks, rocks, drinks, drops her head. I hear a roar of laughter and turn to see Ginny on the path, floating in midstep, her wide eyes staring at me and Grandma sitting, and she's on the verge of tears.

"It's okay," I say. "Go on. Don't miss anything. Grandma's fine." I try to smile.

Her eyes go impossibly wider. "Owen!" she hisses, meaning what, I don't know. Then she runs back up the path to the clearing. A moment later, there's a howl from the kids. More flutes. Clapping. I don't know what is going on. Grandma is just sitting now, as if all the air has been let out of her. She's breathing fast, in-out, in-out. Suddenly, she turns to me, touches my arm.

"You're a good boy."

"Really, should we call Mom?" I ask.

"No!" She pats my arm. "No, no. I'm all better. I get dizzy spells. Tiny spells. Now. Let's see what those non-Indians are up to."

We slowly climb the path to the clearing. In the meantime, Kyle has somehow managed to shift the entire top row in the bleachers so that Grandma and I can just plop down on the end without bothering anyone else. My throat tightens again. Kyle just thinks of things. People are so nice. Ginny turns around, smiles to see Grandma back. They wave to each other. Grandma blows her a kiss, then leans to my ear. "I love you," she whispers.

"What about me?" asks Kyle, a pretend-hurt look on his face.

She cackles. "You too, Kyle, dear. Sean, too. And everyone else!"

And I realize I haven't thought about my best friend all day.

FIFTEEN

Mom goes a little out of her mind when I tell her about Grandma. I still don't have a clear picture of what happened back there, but Mom blames herself and a little bit the newspaper for keeping her late at their office on her first week, to which Grandma says, "Nonsense. It was just a spell," which my mom's face tells me might be something more.

Anyway, Grandma spends the next few days with us, is fine and bouncing around, cheering for Kyle and me at Saturday's ball game, going to church and Ginny's ballet lesson. Most of the rest of the time, we hang out as a family, and it's nice. Dad grills, we have lots of patio time, Grandma has a drink, then another, and reminisces about when she lived on "the old Cape," reads with Ginny, doing voices for all the characters, asks me about karting and

Sean. I tell her he's with his grandparents. She hopes he's having as good a time as we are.

By Tuesday morning, she's ready to go home. We all get long, very long, hugs.

"Oh, I love you, you pixie," she says to Ginny. "Be good."

"I am!" Ginny says. "Grandma, I love you."

"You be good, too," she adds to me. "I know you will be."

Her hands and arms, her shoulders, are just bones, sharper than I realized, and I wonder again whether her spell is something more. She seems smaller than when she came. We take photos of us in various combinations. She kisses Mom and Dad, hops out to her car, beeps, and is off.

"Is Grandma okay?" I ask Mom when the car pulls out onto the road.

She smiles a half smile. "She hasn't been feeling too well lately. She's seeing a doctor." She taps her chest, for me, not for Ginny. Her heart?

"But she's okay," Ginny says as if it's true. Then she frowns and her eyes go wide like at the puppet show. "She is, right?"

"I'll visit her in a few days to make sure," Mom answers.

Dad has been standing at the sink during this, looking into the backyard. Then he turns. "Maybe your mother could come here. We've talked about it before, but maybe now's the time. It's dumb for her to drive back and forth over the bridge so much. We can, I don't know, find a room. Or even build a room."

"Really?" Ginny says. "Yay!"

Mom brightens up. "I'll talk to her again. She didn't want to the last time we said anything. But I'll go this week."

"Good. I think it might work." Dad jangles his pickup keys. "I mean, how long are we . . ." He stops, spins on his heel. "Owen? Track time."

The day starts out overcast, but hot, humid, eighty-four, no wind. Because of Grandma leaving, we're a little late getting there. Jimmy and the boys have opened. The lot is full, the crowd is teeming. I think of all the sticky seats I'll have to rinse off, and I suddenly wonder why I've never counted how many seats I clean each day, each week over the summer.

I like the idea of knowing and start to figure it out mentally, but I don't get much further than "twelve karts times seven races per hour times an average of eight hours a day" before I'm busily running around spritzing. Then, just after I refill the spray bottle, I look and realize the weather is up to something.

It's not quite noon when the sky tips a dark bowl over the track. Everything has turned blue gray. My father looks up. My uncle looks up. They lean and talk about whether to shut down for the day. But without actual rain, you try to keep tracks open as long as you can.

"One more race. We'll see how much darker it gets," my uncle says.

"Agreed," Dad says.

So another race begins, and I'm caught between looking up and being mesmerized by how well my dad fixed the green kart we bought from that guy. It's running fast and weaving through the others, even past number seventeen, which a girl is driving way too slowly, and the whole race is battering the air like a hundred lawn mowers and I'm starting again with "twelve times seven times eight" when a flash of white jackknifes across the sky. It's an enormous, silent, jagged sizzle.

The waiting crowd does a collective "Whoa!" and some of the drivers immediately slow down. But when the crack of thunder hits a few seconds later, one driver, a T-shirted girl who just squeaked in at the height requirement, the driver of number seventeen, in fact, lets out a scream you can hear over everything. Her kart swerves wildly around two others near the turn at the top of the track. She runs over the rear tire of one of them and bounces at top speed toward the fence.

"She's out of control!" somebody yells. I drop my stuff and rush out with the boys, and we all begin waving her down, like cops when you're driving too fast through a construction zone. There's another blast of light and a boom like a bomb going off, and the girl freaks. Her kart slams into a row of orange cones and sends them flying like bowling pins. Her arms and feet seem to freeze as she accelerates right at me. The sky opens, spattering us with quarter-size drops of hot rain.

"Stop, stop, stop!" my father cries, and now he's out there waving his arms, too, but she can't slow down. I jump out of the way to the boardwalk behind me, but I misjudge the step and fall flat on my back. My dad is there, dragging me away as the girl slams into the board-walk full speed. My feet would have been sliced off if Dad hadn't pulled me out of the way.

The seat belt holds the girl snug, and she doesn't look hurt. But she's a disaster—crying, screaming, squirming in her seat—not that you can hear her because the rain is hammering so hard. One of the older kids shuts off her engine from behind and unbuckles her. Everyone's drenched. Her mother pushes through the gate and rushes to the kart, screaming "Sorrysorrysorry!" to me, her hair soaked, rain streaming down her face.

"It's okay," I say, trying to be calm. "It happens." My voice squeaks. I'm shaking, staggering along the boardwalk to the office, and I probably would collapse if my dad didn't have me by the arm.

"Owen, jeez, Owen," he's saying like *he's* the one in shock. We're saturated by the time the karts are back in the garage, where the boys give me an ovation. Most customers huddle under the awning in front of the track's ice cream stand to see if we'll start up again or to get a refund. Some have taken shelter in their cars. The rain keeps spitting bullets.

"How are you?" Dad's face is strained, bloodless. His hands on my shoulders are warm, strong, but shaky.

"I'm all right."

"Are you? You want something. Water? Coffee? Owen, man!" He shakes his head, keeps his hands on me. "That could have gone bad."

"I'm okay. Go. Hand out vouchers."

"Never mind that, Jimmy'll do it."

I slump into his desk chair, quaking but feeling lucid. "I'll regain consciousness in a couple of minutes," I joke.

"Just sit." Dad runs out, grabbing a stack of yellow cards that allow a free ride to the drivers who were pulled in early.

I catch my breath, finally get it back to normal, stand, and trot out through the garage, but it's pretty much all over. The high school boys grin at me, the nearly wounded hero. I help nudge the karts into lines and pull in the "open" banner while my dad and uncle head back to the office to count up three hours of receipts. The track closes, the boys leave, and the parking lot eventually empties out to just my dad's pickup and my uncle's car. I'm totally back to myself by then as I listen to their grumpy talk from the doorway.

It's Cape Cod. We've been through this before. When it storms, go-karts are usually done for the day. After tourists run for shelter, they eat, return to their hotels or rented houses, drive back over the bridge for the indoor karts, give it up for the day, drift away. That is, unless the rain stops and the pavement dries and you can reset, but that usually doesn't happen and it doesn't look like it'll happen today. The sky is black, the rain is pounding the pavement in sheets, and the air is one constant rumble of thunder.

Finally, Dad breathes a heavy sigh. "Okay, Owen, that's it. Let's hit the road."

But my uncle's peering up out the window. "I don't know. It could pass."

"The help's gone home," Dad says.

Uncle Jimmy flips the screen on his cell phone. "It's clearing in Hyannis. Just you and me could run the place for a couple of hours later on. We used to."

Dad leaves me at the door, goes to the window, tilts his head from side to side. "Maybe. You stick here, Jimmy.

Buzz me if you think it's possible. Owen and I are taking off, but I won't be far."

Dad drives us home. We talk about the near miss, and he's saying he's sorry. "We never should have let her out there. She just looked older than her height."

"It's okay. It's almost fun, having a story I can tell people. The lightning exploding overhead. The runaway kart. How I almost died, killed by my own favorite car."

"Dying is a stretch."

"How you leapt over the wall to save me, dragged my lifeless body to safety. The police, the EMS vans . . ."

He laughs. "Yeah, all right. Tell it to Sean that way if you want to, but not your mother. Let me do that. Or maybe not do that."

And Sean's there in my mind again, staring with eyes as black as the sky.

My dad works back up Route 124 in the still-pounding rain, wipers flicking, and I feel my tongue slide around in my mouth. I sense my lips twitching and curling over words that aren't there yet.

Dad, I want to say, and am hoping I can come up with the rest when he says, "You know, I might have to go back this afternoon, if this stops. You don't have to come with me. Some people will pull in, but you know how it is, most will figure we're closed. There won't be a crowd— oh, shoot."

He drops a hand to the front pocket of his jeans. His phone is buzzing. He takes his foot off the gas and leans to the side to dig his phone out, but he can't get to it before it stops. He glances at the screen. "Huh? Oh. It was Sean. Here. Tell him how you died and I brought you back. Put it on speaker."

I don't want to talk to Sean, don't want to call back. Besides, he's at his grandparents' house. He's safe there. But my dad's expecting it, so I tap RECENTS and it shows me the number. Sean's house phone.

He's home from his grandparents'?

"And don't forget the part where we're all dodging lightning bolts to get to you," Dad says. "The go-kart's on fire by this point." He laughs to himself.

It rings three times. I hang up. "No answer."

Twenty thousand times I open my mouth to try to speak, and twenty thousand times I hear Sean say *If you tell, I will kill myself.*

"Drop me there, okay, Dad?"

"Sorry?"

"Sean's. Drop me at Sean's house. He's home."

"You got it."

SIXTEEN

I should be with Shay, right?

He told me something, and if he told only me, then I need to be there to hear more, in case he has to tell me that, too. I don't know. It's a feeling. It isn't logical. There's no way I want to hear any more. I think of being in the fairyland theater, laughing for a few minutes with Kyle. I think about Ginny. About Grandma. About the lightning and the screaming girl in number seventeen.

But soon enough, we're slowing down. When Dad comes to our turn, he puts on his blinker, takes a left instead of a right. My heart beats faster. I see the house. Mrs. Huff's car is in the driveway. Dad pulls in behind it. Thick raindrops splash off our windshield and hood, but not as quickly as before.

He switches the wipers from fast to regular.

"You want me to stick around?"

Not thinking about it, I come out with "Nah," and it nearly sticks in my throat. "I'll walk home. Or if it's still raining, Mrs. Huff will drive me. Or Mom and Ginny will come. It's good."

He leans under the windshield, looks up. "Your uncle might be right. This storm is moving fast. I will have to go back to Harwich. You're sure?"

"Yep. Thanks."

I get out, run up the driveway, crunching shells under my feet. Shay is sitting on the floor of his porch, leaning against the inside wall. I wave to my dad. He leaves. The rain is pooling in the corner of the porch floor, big drops splashing down from the eaves. Sean's pants are soaked through. He's not moving.

"When did you get back?" I ask him.

"Yesterday."

"Why didn't you call me?"

He doesn't answer.

"And why don't you go inside? You're sitting in water."

He doesn't move.

I blurt stuff. "I nearly died at the track. A girl . . ."

But he's saying something. I barely make out his mumbling. "Sean, what?"

"It's different now." His words are so soft, and my blood is thumping in my ears. "It's different."

143

I want to be angry, but I push that down, hoping it doesn't sound in my voice. "Uh-huh. What's different?"

"There's a camera."

I don't want to hear it. A camera now? *Shay, come on!*

"Where is there a camera?" My voice cracks.

"His friend brought a camera."

"You mean his girlfriend?"

"Her?" he growls. "She doesn't know anything. She's a freaking moron."

"She looks okay. Then who? What friend?"

"Carrie may not even be his girlfriend," he goes on, "just somebody he knows. Mom was at the dress store yesterday, firing somebody for stealing, and the police had to be there. He knew that. Paul knew she'd be a long time. He said a friend of his was dropping by, and he had a camera and took videos."

"Of what? I still don't know what you mean—"

"Because you don't want to, Owen." He barks it out quick and low. "Don't be stupid. You're the only one who knows. I have to tell somebody, and you're it. He took pictures of me. Naked and doing stuff. You don't want to know what I did."

As many times as I've tried to picture what happens in his room I haven't been able to. Now in the rain, the whole world of the porch is crying and it seems I can almost see it. I make out a jumble of arms and legs, some small, others hairy, and then hazily I begin to see everything else.

My face grows hot and my skin heavy on me, weighing me down. My chest is sparking, nervous. Is this really happening? I need to go to the bathroom. I want to stand up and run away but can't. Words come out of me. "Paul needs to die."

"He said I was 'cute' in a towel."

The words make my stomach turn.

"He said I was a pretty—a good-looking boy—a little boy, and that when he talked to his friends they said they wanted to see pictures of me and videos because I was young and so white. He made me take my pod off my arm. He has a bunch of friends who like that stuff. It's part of undressing. So they made movies."

"Sean, God! What does that mean?"

"I said, no, I wouldn't. But I did it. He said it was just for his friends. If I tell, the movies will go online and everyone will see me. He said he'll show the movies to the whole world if I tell."

"He forced you to do things?"

"I don't even know." He looks up at me, but not quite at me. Over my shoulder into the rain still beating down. "He didn't hurt me or hit me. He didn't force me. I did things he told me to. He said it's how boys learn and it's fine. He ended up fine. A new car, a big guy at church, a pretty girlfriend. That's what he calls her, but it's not like a regular girlfriend. She's stupid. So I just . . . did what he asked. And after it was over, he . . ."

He stops, his mouth open. He leans over the porch railing and spits into the bushes a few times.

"Sean, he what?"

When he comes back up, his face is gray. "Can we go to Wellfleet again? Your mom said maybe we could."

The words won't form. I watch a couple of cars go by the house. "Look, Shay, I won't tell anybody, but you have to call the police—"

"No."

"You have to."

"No. He said it was just for his friends and only for a little bit. He said he could tell I didn't mind it. But if I told, though, he would know. Then it would go out there and everyone would see." It was a flood now, Sean spilling it all out. "He said his friend sometimes just does it, puts pictures online, and we shouldn't make him mad."

Sean stands and his pants are completely saturated from the rain on the porch. I stand near him under the roof. I have no words. Rain streams a waterfall in front of our faces. Then it lessens, almost suddenly. There's a glimmer of sunlight on the grass; it vanishes, then comes again. His eyes are fixed on the crushed seashells covering the path from the driveway to the house, but he can't be seeing them with those black eyes, the way the bleached bits are catching the light shafting from the clouds. The pockets and puddles of rain drench the shells and make them swim as if they're underwater.

Sean's eyes are blank, staring away, not at anything I can see, maybe at scenes inside his head. If it's what I imagine, it's a nightmare of horrible limbs and hands, and the feelings and pinches and pain of what those men make him do.

His features are twitching, but his head isn't moving. He's biting the inside of his lip hard. I see blood.

"You can't help me," he says. "I have to go."

"Sean, wait. Look, you have to—no, we'll do something next time he comes. We'll stop him, you and me—"

He goes inside.

I stand there looking out—more sunlight is lying over the lawn now, the purple clouds are flying east to Orleans and Eastham—I stand waiting and staring at the shells and the glittering grass, and my vision blurs. I've known Sean since forever. We've done everything together. We're like brothers. So how can this be happening to him and not to me or anybody else? I don't know what to do, except maybe to try to take some of it on myself. The screen door has barely settled shut when it opens again behind me.

"We can do something ourselves," I say. "I don't know what, but we can."

"What don't you know? Do what yourselves?"

It's not Shay in the doorway. It's his mother. I can't answer.

"Owen, he's all wet. What did you two do out here?"

"Oh. No. Nothing. He was sitting."

"Sitting? Do what yourselves? Why are you out here? Come inside."

"No, it's okay."

She looks at me, searches my face. "Well, he's mad about something, and he won't tell me."

I guess my face looks strange, sad, maybe, because she smiles like a mother I might have if I didn't have my own mother. "You boys will work it out, I guess?" She might be waiting for an answer, but she doesn't wait long and starts fidgeting, and already seems somewhere else. Her shop, her worries, money, stealing, whatever. She shifts a big flowery bag from one shoulder to the other. The air is brighter now, the hard rain pretty much over. "Shay went to his room and closed the door. Are things all right with you two?"

I try to make myself smile back. "Sure. I think he's just getting something to show me. Are you going out? Sorry about the shop."

She lets out a sigh. "The shop. We had to fire two girls. You met one. Gee, she called herself, as if that's a name. Anyway, she was in it with another girl. One would steal, the other would cover it up. What a mess. Almost a thousand dollars of merchandise gone, can you believe it? That's what we've found so far. I have to run over to the printer, then back to Provincetown. The new shop flyers are ready."

My ears are buzzing, my head is shaking back and forth.

"The babysitter will be here in a few minutes," she goes on. "Sean probably told you how he hates when I call Paul a babysitter. There should be a different name for them, I guess, when you guys get to a certain age. But sometimes you just need someone older. He does—"

"Don't go." I'm shaking so much I think I'll throw up. "Or, I can stay and watch him do his blood stuff. I know the routine. Before eating. The controller. He showed me. I've been his friend for a long time. Sean wants you to . . . well . . ."

Finally, I don't know what I'm saying.

Her shoulders slump. Her smile goes flat across her face. "It'll be too long, a few hours. This shop, well, I guess all these things have trouble. Some of the time. It'll get better. Anyway, I can't leave you two here alone. What sort of mother would I be? Paul's on his way. You met him, of course you did. You know, it really helps having some-one I can count on to be here." She's rambling like an insane person.

"Sean doesn't need a sitter."

"After the summer, it'll slow down, but now, being there is critical." She looks at the time on her phone. "He should be here soon. I hope . . ."

"The rain's over," I tell her. "Seriously, don't go. You know what? My mom and Ginny can pick up your flyers. Or they can come here. Or Sean can come home with me."

"She can't. Your mother can't. I just spoke with her. She's getting ready to go to your grandmother's, who's not feeling well again. I'm sorry about that. I think she wants you home, to stay with Ginny. Or you are all going to see your grandma? I don't know, Owen. It won't work today."

I stand in the middle of the top step as if I'm trying to stop her from leaving. The sun is splashed on the lawn now and glistening. "My dad can come back. He's not at the track yet."

Her eyes search the street. "Maybe next time. Good, there's Paul driving around the corner. You know, I really don't think Sean is coming out. Maybe you should be getting home, or go with your mom to visit your grand-mother? I don't know, Owen. Please. Paul isn't comfortable handling kids if he doesn't have their parents' okay. I'll drop you at your house. Sean's not coming out."

It's going too fast. It's out of control. I can't do anything to stop it.

Paul pulls up. He's alone. No Carrie this time. He's smiling when he stops, but by the time he closes the car

150

door behind him and sees me, his smile is gone. It's stupid, but I feel as if I'm naked now.

"Owen is just going home," Mrs. Huff says, moving her arm around my shoulders, then quickly removing it and hopping down the stairs next to me. "Sean's in his room. Owen, this is Mr. Landis."

"Paul, please," he says, "and yes, we've met before. Owen, how are you?"

He smiles like anybody else. I search his face and eyes to see what I can see. No clue to anything. He puts out his hand. It's wet. Probably from the car door. The thought of his wet fingers turns my stomach, but I shake hands anyway.

"I'm okay."

"Good, good. Fabulariffic," he says, in the dumb way he talks.

I scan up and down the street to see if another car is coming—his friend, the one with the camera. But there isn't.

"Okay, then," Mrs. Huff says. "Paul, I have tomorrow off, so Sean and I are good, but can you make it from Thursday on for a few days?"

"*Naturellement*, Mrs. H. And Owen Todd, I'll see you around, all right?"

Him using my last name creeps me out. I don't know if I answer, but Shay's mom is already near her car, late for her printer, so I follow her across the wet shells, get in, and latch on the belt. She flicks the wipers two, three times to clear the rain from the windshield. I glance over at Sean's room, the corner room on the right. His window shade is down.

Backing out, she sets the car in drive and turns the wheel while Paul bounces up the steps and into the house.

Stop the car! Mrs. Huff, stop the car right now! I want to say.

But my mouth won't open. I don't say anything.

SEVENTEEN

"Some storm, wasn't it?" Mrs. Huff waves her hand across the windshield.

She drives neither fast nor slow, but somehow without me noticing, we're already at the corner. Shay's house is out of the mirror now, hidden, faraway, as if it's in another town.

If you tell, I will kill myself.

"I'm so glad we got a new roof on the house," she goes on. "That downpour would have drowned us."

Forget the storm! Paul is hurting Sean! He's doing bad, horrible things to him. Stop!

"Sean's room especially. Water once seeped down the walls from the attic and stained the paint and smelled bad until winter and the furnace heat dried it up." She talks fast, like a robot. "You know that smell. We all do. It's Cape Cod."

Stop the car! You need to help Sean. He's being tortured!

"Our builder said if we waited any longer we'd be in real trouble."

Iron weights press on my tongue. It's turned to stone in my mouth. I can't pry my stupid lips apart. She points to a garden we pass, presses a button, and my window slides down. Big blue balls of petals droop from a hedge onto the sidewalk.

"Hydrangeas. I love the blue. The rain really clobbered them."

How can I say the words I should say? *Help Sean!* They don't have anything to do with flowers or rain or roofs. They don't work in this suddenly sunny world.

I will kill myself.

I know he knows how. Sean doesn't need a gun. Or poison. Or a rope. He can just swim out where it's too deep. Or inject himself with his backup pen so his body floods with too much insulin. He'll go into shock, into a coma, die. What if I just tell her *Sean is sad*? That would be enough, wouldn't it?

Instead, I blurt out, "I think my mom's taking Ginny and me shopping on Thursday. Shay could come with us. Tell him I'll call him tomorrow, okay?"

She slows in front of my house, pulls to the curb.

"Sounds great. I won't cancel Paul until you know for sure, but I'll tell Sean. He'll like that."

―――――――――

I get out of the car, run inside. My mother says she doesn't want Ginny and me to go to Grandma's house with her, because it's mostly to do errands, medical errands, it could be a lot of waiting, she says. For the first time ever she leaves me in charge at home. I'm a babysitter now.

I suddenly wish we had school during the summer. It wouldn't be just me anymore. Teachers, counselors, lunch monitors, all of them could tell something was wrong, couldn't they? Shay's mother is too busy, with too much on her mind, always far away, but they'd see it. They'd know. They would. But summer is different. It's only us. The huge crowds of tourists and beach people and renters couldn't care less about us. We're just "the locals" to them. No, this summer there's only Sean and his busy mom and my busy parents and Paul Landis. And me.

―――――――――

That evening, Mom is still out. Dad's back, and another storm roars through, dumping three inches of rain on us in just the first two hours. It's the tail end of the system,

I overhear the television guy saying, and it will take us through the morning, when the sun will burst back. The rosy bum of summer, my grandmother would say. It will be eighty and dry.

I can't stand the TV noise. I go to my room. I open the window a crack. Gashes of lightning are followed by cracking thunder. Ginny pokes her head in my room, asks about Grandma. I say, "I don't know any more than you do."

"You should," she says. She's still looking at me, then adds, "Mom won't be back until late."

"I know."

"Dad's making popcorn."

"So what?" I say more harshly than I mean. I want to come back with "Ginny, I'm sorry," but I don't get it out before she snaps, "Poop!" and slams my door. I can't manage to get up off my bed to go after her. It's not Ginny or Grandma now, or Mom or Dad. It's Sean I have to think about.

Trees sway in the yard, the rain fires down on the roof over my room, then batters the windowpanes sideways, as if it's trying to get in. My walls are dry. I try to breathe the air of the storm, sniffing at the opening between the sash and the windowsill. I can't get anything into my lungs. They hurt. I want to cry.

The wind is saying *O-O-O* over and over and the

lightning is flashing in my eyes and something changes. If there are iron weights on my stupid tongue, there's a ball of something just as heavy and big that's also inside me. Only it's lower and deeper, and it's getting bigger. It's a ball of hate, and it wants to come out.

If I can't speak, I'll do something anyway. I'll do the only thing I can do without blowing up the whole world.

I'll go to Shay's house when Paul is there. I'll hide somewhere, I don't know where, but I'll see for myself. If it's all been Sean's stories up till now, it won't be a story anymore.

I'll see and I'll have proof and it'll be proof for everybody else too, because it won't be just him and me.

The ball of hate inside me grows, filling my throat, closing it. It's hate for the babysitter. Hate for what he's doing to Sean. Hate that I have to do something to save a kid from a grown-up.

The ball of hate says only one thing.

Do it, Owen, do it.

First, I need a phone. Mom's or Dad's? Mom always keeps hers close. She gets calls, makes calls. Dad's is mostly for business. He goes hours without using it. He has one day a week off from the track, sometimes Wednesday, sometimes Thursday. This week it's Thursday, which is perfect. Mrs. Huff asked Paul to sit for Sean. Forget about going shopping. I won't even ask Mom. I'll go to Sean's house. I'll do it then. It's coming together. I have a plan. I know what to do.

I wait it out until Mom gets home. It's late. Ginny goes to sleep, I can't.

"Grandma's all right for now," she tells me and Dad when she finally gets in. "She's been on a couple of heart medications she wasn't telling us about. But she's going to the hospital Thursday for tests, and I'm going with her. We figured that out together with her doctor today. I hope she'll start to feel better soon."

Dad hugs her. So do I.

"I'll tell Ginny in the morning," I say. "I have to talk to her anyway."

I do. I apologize and tell her I have a lot of things going on. "Boy stuff," I say. She scrunches up her face as if what I said was icky, but then says, "Okay. I unpoop you." We're good again.

I wait Wednesday. Sean's mother has the day off. I don't know why. I don't care. He's safe. The sun came, but by afternoon it's raining again, and practice is canceled. Besides being on the phone with Grandma at least three times during the day, Mom tries to fill the minutes between now and when she goes back to her with errands. She decides to take Ginny and me shopping a day early. She says I need new shorts. Fine. New shorts. It doesn't matter anyway, because I have a plan. I work it over and over in my mind as we go from store to store, and though the idea of going to Sean's when Paul is there terrifies me, I work it so many times it seems simple.

Do it, Owen, do it.

Then something crashes down that I should have seen coming but didn't.

It's just before supper Wednesday evening.

I'm trying on my new shorts after a shower. Every time I get dressed or undressed I think of what Sean told me. Then I hear my mom suddenly sob into the phone. "Oh, my gosh, no!" I run down to the kitchen. She's staring out the window and turns to me, still holding the phone. Her face is white, her eyes red and wet and burning into mine.

"Your grandmother," she says, "she di—she died."

"What? No," I say stupidly. "No! She was just here. You were just there! The doctor, the tests? What happened? No," I say, and, "No, Mom, no!" All of which is meaningless. What *do* you say? You try to deny it. It's idiotic. You try to *explain* how something that just happened couldn't happen, that it's impossible.

Except it isn't. I should have seen it, the skinny shoulders, the emergency at the puppet show, her wobbly tiny little body. I sit next to Mom at the table as she listens glassy-eyed to someone, Grandma's doctor maybe, or one of her neighbors, I don't know who. It's a low voice, technical, long sentences, so a doctor or a nurse or someone at a hospital.

"How did it happen?" I whisper.

Mom shakes her head. "It was sudden. She simply . . . fell."

"Fell? How do you fall and just—"

Mom stands up from the table, shakes her head, puts her finger in her ear to hear the caller. "Repeat that, please?" She listens to another long string of words. "I'll be there as soon as I can. Yes. Thank you."

"Mom?"

She turns, her eyes streaming. "It was probably a heart attack. Maybe a stroke. In Macy's in the mall near there. They have to do . . . They'll find out later." Then all she can say is "My mommy!" She cries on my shoulder. Something in my chest collapses and I feel drained and empty. My throat seizes as I hug her. Now is the time to let my mom hug me for as long as she wants. Everything's dripping inside me. My eyes sting with tears. We hold each other until she pulls away.

"I have to call Daddy. We have to go to Hanover."

Minutes later, she's just connected to my dad at the track when Ginny comes running in, whistling "O Little Town of Bethlehem." She's wearing her Peter Pan shorts and the new bright-red T-shirt she got today. She looks like a Christmas card. Mom gives me a glance. Right. She's just about to tell my dad and doesn't want Ginny to learn that way.

"Hey, come here," I say.

"Why are you crying? Why is Mom crying?" But she follows me into the living room. "What's going on?"

I want to say anything but the truth because I know she'll go nuts, but that's stupid and rude. Mom's voice cracks loudly in the kitchen. Ginny's looking back and forth from the kitchen to me, and then stares at me the way she did when Grandma was sick at the puppet play, mouth open, thinking something's wrong, ready to shriek.

I say, "I don't know. We have to go to Hanover for a couple of days, I think."

She looks all over my face for what that might mean, then shakes her head as if to say *"What?"* but not saying that, not saying anything.

"Grandma," I say. "She was sick when we saw her. Sicker than we thought she was. Remember at the puppet show? Well . . . today she . . . passed away."

"Owen!" she screams, just like at the theater. She pushes me with both hands. "Owen?" I try to put my arms around her shoulders, like Mom just did to me, but Ginny tears into the kitchen shouting and hears Mom say ". . . plan the service at her church . . ." Then the phone is back in its cradle, and Ginny crumples into my mother's arms.

I think about the last days with Grandma, and her small

wrinkled hands, and a black space opens up and I see it everywhere like floaters taking over my eyes. I can't get rid of them. My head feels light. Ginny is squirming on the kitchen floor now, angry. Mom on her knees, trying to comfort her, saying to me, "I'd like to go soon, in the morning, first thing. Your aunt and uncles are driving down. It'll be a couple of days, maybe more. Owen, maybe call your coach?"

And my world comes back. "Sure, Mom."

It's only then, after all that, when I'm back upstairs, dialing Coach on the upstairs phone and leaving a message about missing the game on Saturday, that I realize my plan for Sean has been blown off the rails. He doesn't know it, of course. No one knows it but me, but it means more days of doing nothing to help him. I try to figure out how long I'll be away, but I don't know how long it takes when someone dies. Mom's siblings live in Maine, a bit of a drive, so they'll be around for a while. Then I think to call Kyle about what happened because he was with us at the show.

He listens quietly. "Owen, man," he says. "I'm sorry. She was so funny. I liked her a lot."

"I know. She liked you, too. Thanks."

"I was really thinking I'd see her again, lots this summer."

"Yeah, sorry."

"Good thing she was just here, right? I guess she was sick, and we didn't know how bad."

"She kept being funny," I say.

"Funerals are tough. Call me when you get back." And he's so calm and kind I want to start crying again.

Finally, I can't put it off anymore. I call Sean. It's suppertime now. It rings four times. He picks up.

"Hey, Shay. Look, bad news. I have to go to a funeral."

"Mine?" he says.

"Not funny," I whisper into the phone.

He snorts. "'Cause if it's mine, make sure I'm wearing sunglasses." He laughs as if it's a joke, then says, "Just kidding, what's up?" because maybe his mother's near the phone. I hear her voice in the background. I clear my throat.

"My grandmother died today. We're all going to Hanover. She wants to be . . . to be buried with my grandfather in the cemetery there. I have to go."

"Oh, sorry. She was old, though, right?"

"Not that old. No. When did you last see her?"

"I don't remember. Heart attack?"

"No. I don't know. A stroke maybe. Or a heart attack. Mom's not sure. She fell in a store. Macy's in Kingston, she told me. They think it might have been a stroke, but we'll know later. Ginny's a mess. Grandma was a good person. She always liked you, you know."

"Yeah. Sorry. When? When are you going?"

"In the morning. The funeral is Friday. Maybe I'll be home Saturday, maybe not."

Then he says, "Sorry. Those things are gross. I mean, I've never been to one, but I guess they are—wait. Tomorrow and Friday? Oh. I thought we were going shopping. My mom told me."

"Yeah, I was going to ask you to hang out with us tomorrow, but . . ." I just drift off.

A long breath from the phone. "*He's* coming tomorrow and Friday and every day for a while. Never mind. You've got all this stuff to do." I feel the crash in his voice. It's like he's been punched. The air goes totally out of him. He swears into the phone.

"Shay, you have to tell somebody about what Paul is doing."

"I did! I did. And now you have to shut up about it or you know what."

"Stop saying that!" I can't be loud on the phone or someone will hear. Sean swears a few more times. He never used to. My grandma always said he was brought up in a good house, and it's true. He was. But his house isn't good anymore. The bad guys have found a way inside.

"Sorry, Shay," I tell him. "I'll call you when I can." But he's already hung up.

EIGHTEEN

Grandma died and I can't go through with my plan to spy on Paul. It hits me that it doesn't matter that I can't control it. It doesn't matter, because what's the difference between not being able to go and simply not going? Nothing. I can't go, or I don't go, it's all the same for Sean.

I've failed him, either way.

And again that idea that makes you crazy, that any dumb, stupid freak thing—being late for a puppet show, a lightning strike, somebody falling in a store—can bomb your plans to hell. I scream inside. I shriek.

But no, no. I'll go next time Sean is tortured. That's plenty good enough.

———————

We get up early Thursday morning. No one slept. After being all packed the night before, Ginny now starts taking stuff out of her roller bag and putting in other things, then taking them out and staring into the empty suitcase.

Dad tries to help her pack for real, but she starts thrashing around, saying "Grandma! Grandma!" and stomping her feet, so Mom takes over.

"Come on, honey. We have to do this."

I keep looking at the clock, wondering if Paul Landis is at Sean's already.

We finally get on the road at half past nine. On the way we pass through Kingston. There are signs for the Macy's where Grandma had her stroke. Ginny is quiet by this time, doesn't see the signs, probably doesn't even know about Grandma and the store. I hope the casket isn't open. Mom said it might be, that she wanted it to be, at least for us. I've never seen a dead person before. They didn't let me see Grandpa because I was too young, I guess.

First we meet up with my mom's relatives at a hotel. She has two brothers and a sister, all younger than her. We don't see them often because it's a five-hour drive to Maine. My aunt has twin babies. For a while Ginny perks up about seeing them, then gets sad. My uncles have no kids yet.

I don't know why our family doesn't stay in touch more.

Five hours isn't that far, after all. Maybe they didn't get along as kids, my mother and the rest of them. As far as I can tell, my aunt has put herself in charge of stuff, including the funeral arrangements, while her husband, a guy who doesn't say much, deals with the babies.

There's a wake at the funeral parlor that afternoon. Grandma's coffin is closed. I'm relieved. There is an early rush of Grandma's neighbors and old friends. I shake hands with mostly old women. Maybe this means their husbands are dead, like Grandpa died before Grandma did. I look at the clock on the wall as I stand in line with relatives, and I realize it's been hours since I've been to the bathroom. I excuse myself. By the time I get back, the room has thinned out, and I find the flowers are making me retch. I stifle it. There is a wide curtain hung from the ceiling behind her. It's pleated and ruffly like a theater curtain. I think of Grandma on the risers, on the path. Ginny's just sitting next to Mom, leaning into her. Her little face is red, her eyes puffy. I sit on her other side, and she switches to leaning on me. After two hours of up and down and shaking hands and being hugged by strangers, I'm exhausted. I can't control my own thoughts.

Then this.

A handful of my mom's old friends come in, and the minute she goes to talk to them, Ginny sits up. "You're mad at Mommy," she whispers to me.

"What? No, I'm not. Why?"

"Because of Grandma. Mommy went to take care of her, but she died anyway."

"What? No. That's not . . . No, Grandma was sicker than anyone thought."

"Not me? You're not mad at me?"

"Ginny, of course not."

"Then Sean."

I look at her. She's twisting a tissue in her fingers and looking back at me. Big eyes, like my dad's, but so red now. "Not mad. It's different. A little mad, maybe. It's mostly something else, something different."

"Boy stuff?"

"Yeah."

She inserts the end of the tissue in my nostril and I snort it out, and she starts laughing softly. It's nervous, odd to hear, but she's beyond exhausted and can't stop laughing until my mother hurries back and puts her arms around her and it turns into crying.

While the other families stay in a hotel they booked, we spend the night at Grandma's little house in Hanover. It smells like her. Not a bad odor, like stuffiness or mothballs or stale breath, but the homey, close, old-person smell she usually had. I pack it in early, wasted, but assured that tomorrow might not be as bad or as long. First the church, then the reception. Ginny is conked out on the other side

of the room on a folding cot my dad found and made up
with fresh sheets and pillows. I don't mind being in a
bedroom with my little sister. While she's snortling, I lie
awake and imagine that Sean's day is over, too.

———————————

The morning's not better. It's worse.

After thinking we're going straight to the church, I
hear we're going back to the funeral parlor to pick up
Grandma's body. Not actually pick up, of course, but we're
going to follow the hearse to the church.

Ginny's in a strange mood, often looking at me with
those searching eyes, but not saying very much. Then
Mom lobs a bombshell.

"We're going to take one last look at Grandma," Mom
says. "To say good-bye."

"Look at Grandma? Mommy?" says Ginny. Again, my
mother's arm is around her shoulders.

Dad smiles a sad smile at me, shrugs with his face.
He's been quiet through the whole thing mostly, dry-
eyed. His face is gray, though, and I can tell he's sinking
under the sadness and suddenness. He lost his mother
when he was small.

We go into the parlor. It's the same as last night. The
flowers are still full of scent and maybe more now that

they're aging. The coffin lid is open. No one but the funeral-home guys are there, all in black suits.

Mom goes straight to the casket and kneels in front of it, looking in. She prays, then makes the sign of the cross. Dad kneels next to her, his arm around her shoulders. While I watch them, Ginny goes to Mom's side and looks in the casket. Her little pocketbook drops to the floor. Mom pulls a limp Ginny to her, folds her into herself. Dad gets up, Mom shifts, Ginny kneels. All this is silent. I think of myself, too young to be there for my grandfather's funeral. Ginny's maybe a year older than I was then.

A long few minutes pass. Mom makes another sign of the cross, and Ginny repeats it. Dad looks out the window. It's a great big sunny day. I wonder if he's thinking about the track. But no, he's not a jerk. He's here with us, or with his own mother, which is okay.

One of the undertakers looks at me, a kindly look, I think. He waves me forward. Another man takes his hands from his pockets, checks his watch.

It's time.

I don't want to, but I go to the kneeler. I look down and see my grandmother, white as snow, shrunken into the silky fabric, tinier than I've ever seen her, her face relaxed, her wrinkles, some of them, smoothed out, her thin hair wafted up and styled. She's wearing a pink dress, a little string of pearls around her neck. Her hands are folded heavily over her waist. She is a white stone statue made up with a human face that I'm glad I saw alive so recently. The insides of my own face, throat, and chest are gushing.

"I love you, Grandma." I make the sign of the cross and get up. My dad's hand is on my shoulder. The undertakers move in, smile questioningly at us, at Mom, then close the coffin. The waving guy waves us to the door and into the waiting limousine.

There aren't too many people at church. Mom's brothers, along with my dad and the undertakers, carry the casket up the church steps to a rolling stand, which they usher to the altar rail. The priest seems to know who my grandmother was, says a few words about her, how she loved her family, the knitting club, the garden club. Mom and my aunt sit in the pew while their brothers give short speeches. I remember nothing of what they said but a few funny things Grandma did when they were small, and the laughter of her friends in the congregation. All in all, the service is short. The summer choir's thin and raggedy, like at Old Sailors.

In the car again, we leave the parking lot for one final ride.

Ginny is quivering. I find myself twisting a tissue and

trying to put it in her nose, but she swats it down, staring out the front at the hearse driving ahead of us.

"Where is Grandma going now?"

"Heaven," my mom says. "But she'll still be with us."

"She's always with us," Dad says. "In our hearts." It's strange to hear him say this kind of thing. "We can think about Grandma every day."

"No. She's in the black station wagon. Where is she going?"

"To the cemetery," I whisper to her. "Remember?"

"Oh, right. After church is the cemetery. Then we go home?"

"First, lunch with your uncles and aunt," Mom says.

"And the babies?"

"And the babies. Then we go home."

Ginny yawns. "I remember now."

At the cemetery the priest mostly reads from a prayer book, then blesses the casket, but it doesn't go into the ground. Afterward, Mom's brothers take us out for a big meal. Besides us, there are a few people who I saw at the funeral home and some from the church. My aunt and mother have lots to drink. It's nearly suppertime now and it seems to be going on too long, and I think of Sean at home. I ask my mom for her cell to call him. I know enough not to ask for Dad's, because if I ever *do* go to Sean's with it, I don't want him remembering I asked for it now.

I go out to the lobby to make the call. He picks up on the third ring.

"Hello, Mrs. Todd," he says when he picks up.

"Shay, it's just her phone."

He laughs. "I figured."

He sounds okay, not depressed or mad like Wednesday.

"Are you all right?" I ask.

"What do you mean?"

He sounds normal. Or, not normal, exactly. But I almost feel us going back to the time before any of this happened. "Is . . . he there?"

"Who?"

"Who. Paul. The babysitter."

A pause on the line. "Yeah. It's just the usual Friday. Nice day. We're out in the backyard. How's the funeral? I mean, it's sad, right? It's probably sad? Without you at the game tomorrow, I feel like we'll win. Ha-ha. Too bad you won't see my home run. Home run*ssss*, plural. Blam, blam, blam!"

I wonder if I'm hearing him right or, for a second, if it's even him on the phone. Then I guess that he's talking like this because Paul is listening. I scan the dining room. People are talking quietly, some of them. Others are drinking. A lot are drinking, especially my aunt, who somehow finds it possible to whoop a big laugh. Three or four ancient people have nearly disappeared into their chairs, surrounded by somebody's grandchildren.

"There was a lot of crying. At first. My mother, mostly, and my aunt and one of the two uncles. My dad's pretty quiet and tired and probably wants to get home. Me, too. Ginny was all right. Pretty good, actually. No one's happy."

"That's tough. I gotta go. Someone's at the door."

"What? Who's there? Don't let him in—"

The phone clicks off.

NINETEEN

I can't wait to get home, but it's already mid-morning on Saturday by the time we hit the road. Mom and her sister and brothers made a big promise to get together more often, talking about driving routes to where they live in Maine. Ginny's happy about that because she'll get to play with the babies again, and even, as she says, "watch them grow up," which strikes me both as mature for a five-year-old and a little strange.

Now, I'm in the back of the car, with Ginny zonked out and sleeping next to me. Mom is leaning her head against the window, probably under the weather. Dad is at the wheel, driving jerkily, stop and go, so slow because it's a weekend. A hard overnight rain has left the highway puddled. Even though it's now steaming away and the sky is clearing, the lanes are packed, and it takes us two and a half hours from Hanover.

It's early afternoon when we get home. The ball game is long over. Last night's clouds hang above Brewster like a ragged gray shelf, but a breeze is finally pushing them on their way east.

I know what I need to do. All the way in the car I've been planning the route through the yards to Sean's house, skulking across lawns and past hedges in my mind.

By the time I change it's near two. Mom's gone out for groceries. Dad is cutting the lawn. Ginny's sitting at the patio table, watching him mow crisscross stripes. He wants to be at work, but my uncle insisted he take another day, which Dad argued into a half day, so he's home for a little longer. He's wearing a floppy hat, filthy cutoff jeans, a T-shirt, ratty work shoes. A plastic bag is sticking out of his back pocket, in case he finds something—cat poop, deer droppings—that he needs to pick up before the mower mashes it.

"I'm going to Shay's," I say to Ginny.

"Mom is at the store for food," she says.

"I know." I soften that. "Thanks."

On the tabletop in front of her are a coloring book and a box of colored pencils, both closed.

I sit down on the bench next to her, terrified about what I'm planning to do, but Ginny's staring glassy-eyed at the lawn like a zombie, not seeing Dad rolling the mower over it, not seeing anything. It's a look that reminds me of Sean.

"Grandma was pretty great, wasn't she?" I say, opening the box of pencils, drawing one out. "I mean, she loved going to the puppet show. The ball games. Ballet. She liked hanging out with us. I bet she loved your dancing. She probably told you she did."

Ginny's chin quivers. She blinks. Her eyes are moist.

"You know, Gin, what Mom and Dad said was true. Grandma's always with us, if we keep thinking about her. She's here right now—"

"I don't want anybody else to die." She bows her head like she's praying, then crashes into me, and I wrap my arms around her. She's so soft and small; I forget sometimes how small. I'm shaking as much as she is, and my head is pounding.

"No one will," I whisper to her. I feel her nod against my chest. "I promise, no one will." She keeps nodding, then sits up and looks out. I see now that Dad has paused at the far end of the yard, the mower going, but he's not moving, only looking across the half-cut grass at us. I take a breath. I stand.

"I'll be back in a sec."

She nods. "You promised, remember?"

"I remember."

I dash upstairs to my parents' room. I know my dad will shower after mowing, and he's got his J&D T-shirt and his jeans laid out on the bed. I scoop his phone off the nightstand. Twenty-two percent power. Jeez, Dad! But there's no time to recharge. I turn off the sound, so any calls or incoming texts won't ring.

Then I stop. I stop.

I'm so close to telling, you'd hate me. I hate myself. I could yell down to the yard right from the window I'm looking out. I could tell the whole thing to my dad in a half second. It doesn't matter that Ginny is there. It shouldn't matter when things like this are happening.

I run downstairs. I step onto the back landing. Sunlight breaks over the patio. I yell it in my head, using a word I've never said before but now I find is the only word ugly enough to tell what is going on.

"Dad, Sean is being raped!"

He sees me on the patio next to Ginny and senses something is not right. He stops the mower. I know he hates to do that. He's busy and wants to get the yard done and I know it's hard to restart the mower when it's hot, but he stops it because he senses something, the way I stand, the look on my face, whatever.

"Owen? What?"

I stare at him, sweating, quaking, my head swimming, drowning.

"Sean . . ." I start, then stop.

"Yes?"

Ginny turns from her coloring book, open now, and looks me in the eye.

All I hear in my head is *I will kill myself,* and I can't tell them the truth. What going over to Sean's house will do, I'm not sure, but all I say is "I'm going to Sean's."

Dad knows something is off, but not what. "Mom'll be back soon."

"Like I told you," Ginny says.

"Thanks, I know. I won't be long."

A pause as Dad and I look at each other across the grass before he adds, "Lock the front door when you leave. Half hour, that's all."

I wave. He pulls the mower's cord. It takes him three tries. The motor rumbles to life. He waves. It's over.

TWENTY

Two thirty. The gray sky is half gone, the day is turning perfect blue, with a vast widening sky in the west, drifting waves of salt air, the aroma of cut grass, the scent of roses along our front fence, the crunch of crushed shells.

Except I see hear smell none of it.

I thread through the yards and backyards, cross one, two streets. The air is warm. The steamy pavements are nearly dry. More backyards. Another street. The route is taking me so much longer than it should. I wave blindly to neighbors, all out now because the rain is past. They nod. I barely register the warm-cool-warm as I pass from sun to shade to sun. I creep like a spy. Or a boy who's betraying his best friend.

I see Ginny's eyes.

I see Dad. *Owen? What?*

I see Shay's face in my mind. *It's just for a little while.*

My legs thud along the paths between houses, any one of which might be broken into, but no, only Sean's has been. Maybe it's his fault. He does what they tell him. Scratching through the long grass in the lot for sale two houses down from his, I get angry with him. With him? Or with Paul? Or with myself? That ball of hate is stuck in my throat now. I'm angry about what things have done to me. Making me think things. Making me do things I don't want to. Making me a liar. Except no, that's wrong. All I know is how the hate chokes me.

My feet keep me moving.

A hedge two houses from Sean's house surprises me. It's thick with beach roses, white and papery, and the scent reminds me of Wellfleet. I see his wet, dark face in my mind, hair matted on his forehead. I'm dizzy with not breathing. I suck in heavy, hot air.

I move along the hedge.

There it is. His house. I'm at the far corner of his back-yard, out of sight of his window. I dart along the edge of the yard, glance around the front. Paul's sickening green car is in the driveway. There's a blue car across the street, parked the wrong way. Is that the friend? I check the time on my dad's phone. 2:41. My mom's gonna be home soon, or is already. Quickly. Do this quickly. I edge along the side to the back. Sean's room is on the far side of the house.

I hear nothing. No sounds from inside. The nearest mower sputters to a stop. The only sound now is the shiny drill of insects. I lean out around the patio. I see the window of his bedroom.

My heart skips. I really want to run home and into my dad's arms, but my feet are planted in the grass. I wait, I watch. I want anything but this. Can I just peek in the window? Can I look in? I watch, I wait. Time stops.

Then it doesn't.

Do it, Owen, do it.

The shade is halfway up, halfway down against the sun. Sean's house doesn't have air-conditioning, so the sash is open. The shade flutters. Not a lot. There's a window box of rain-battered flowers outside his room. It'll hide me if I sneak under it. All the other windows in the house are black.

I scurry across the patio and nearly trip, finally slipping to my knees on the grass under the window of his room. I crouch, breathing through my mouth to silence the panting. I could die here, my heart might explode. That would solve something. But I don't die. I breathe and breathe and listen. No sounds. Is anyone even in his room? Is Sean at home? I rise up slowly on my knees. The window box of droopy geraniums is a foot above me.

Then I hear a cough, I don't know whose, and a voice, soft but distinct.

"Take it."

"I don't want to."

My God, it's Sean. A little voice, so little. I want to scream.

"What did I tell you about that, huh? Give me your hand."

It's Paul Landis. His voice is soft but sharp.

"Give me both your hands."

"No!" Sean is farther away when he says this. They are moving around the room. His voice is watery, slippery, as if he's been sobbing.

"Don't be funny now." Paul moves something across the floor. A chair. The nightstand. "You liked it last time."

The words twist my stomach. I want to see what's going on, but not see it. I can guess and not guess. I stretch up as high as I can on my knees. I could slide up slowly and hear more, except I'd bean my head on the flower box. Sean can stand straight up under it, but not me. I realize then that the only way I'll be able to see anything is to get around the side of the stupid flower box. Carefully, I stand on my feet, flat against the clapboards, my knees bent, my head angled under the window frame. I smell the rain-soaked soil in the box and the strong scent of geraniums.

"That's a good one. A real good one. That's more like it."

How words can mean different things. I remember

Coach calling those same words to Kyle on the field a few weeks back. I nearly puke now.

Shifting my feet, I pull my head out from under the box. It's on the level of the sill. Beyond the green stems and leaves, I see something moving in the room. Standing completely still, not breathing, I wait for the next thing to move.

And there they are.

The cheeks of a man's butt.

I nearly scream—but I jam my eyes closed for a second, and the urge passes. I unjam my eyes. The butt— it's Paul's, big and round and rosy and fatter than I thought it would be—is deeper in the room now. He is hunched over, moving toward the corner like he's hunting. I can't see beyond Paul. Then an arm flies out from the corner. Sean's. He doesn't have a shirt on. He doesn't have any clothes on. Something hot jabs my throat. I feel hot pee on my leg, but I don't care. I want to tear the window open and kill that creep for hurting Sean when I hear the other voice.

"Tell him to stop crying. Make him stop crying, and kneel him down on the floor." It is a low voice from a part of the room I can't see.

My throat fills with acid. I can barely stand. Not Sean, please, not Sean. I swear inside my head a million different words in a fraction of a second and tug my dad's phone from my pocket, knowing again how mad he's going to be when he can't find it. I swipe it open and set the camera to video. I press the ON button and hold the phone up to the window, slowly tilting it from side to side, hoping I get something more than soggy geraniums.

"Sean, I think you know what to do now, right?"

"Please, no." He is crying, swatting at Paul, the slap of hands on pudgy flesh. I stop rotating the camera and point it where I think the voices are coming from.

"Sean, I think you know. You can have your pod back in a minute."

Sean sniffles a bunch of times. "Okay."

"And a smile, all right? A big smile. My friends are going to love you."

TWENTY-ONE

My arm is a thing as heavy as lead, but I keep it raised, keep the phone going, keep it filming. I want to run home screaming, but I'm mute, shaking and shivering.

The other guy is saying stuff. I don't hear all of it, but his voice is sharp, cutting. He swears at Sean or Paul or both of them. "Come on!"

"He's a boy," Paul says.

"I don't care, Paul. He was better last time. You said he was ready for more. All this junk takes time to edit out!"

The sound of a hand slapping the wall. I think of rain streaming down it. If I yell, Paul's angry friend could hurt Sean or come after me. My breath roars in my ears, so I stop breathing.

After another long minute, maybe two, I pull the phone back and shrink away, shrink away while my best friend is tortured. I know I have to see if I have anything on the phone, but I can't do that anywhere but at home. At the last second, I take a trembling shot of the two cars on the street, but a screen door squeaks open somewhere and I run through a hedge and away.

Mom is there when I get home, food on the table. Ginny is assembling a sandwich with her fingers the way she packed her suitcase, putting slices of things on, then taking them off. My dad is steaming, storming through the rooms. "I need it when I'm there and now I find out two of the kids called in sick so I have to go!"

I stare at them blindly, stupidly, as Dad calls his cell from the house phone, can't hear it as it vibrates silently in my pocket, then slams the receiver back in its cradle. "Someone took it. If I left it in the track office, Jimmy would answer, so someone took it. But no. I had it upstairs. I thought I did."

Mom tries it now from her cell phone and shakes her head. "Still voice mail."

"I have to go to the bathroom," I say and pass through the kitchen. I run upstairs and stop by my room to pick up my earbuds. I go in the bathroom and quietly slip the door latch I never use.

Nine percent power. I play the video back.

At first there are huge blobs of green and red, then a crisscross of window screen, then it darkens. That was when I held it against the screen. There is Sean's desk. His dresser. Then there is Sean. His white arms and shoulders. Then there is his desk again. Then his naked back. I miss what happens next, it's just twitching back and forth. Finally, the jerking stops. There are Sean and Paul. The camera saw what I couldn't.

Now I see.

TWENTY-TWO

I tell.

I burst out of the bathroom, run downstairs into the kitchen where Ginny is still picking stuff off her bread and Dad is still ranting about his stupid phone.

"Ginny, g-go upstairs," I say, my voice cracking.

"What? No. Did you pee in your pants—"

"Take your sandwich, please, and go to your room."

"Owen, that's rude," my mom snaps.

"Ginny! Go!" I scream. My dad's staring at me, then sees his phone in my hand as Ginny runs from the kitchen, her tongue stuck out at me. She stomps upstairs.

"Owen, what the hell!" Dad says, reaching for the phone.

Even as I think I don't know how to say it and the words can't possibly come out of my mouth, I scream it.

I scream that ugly word I could never bring myself to say.

"Sean is being raped! He's being raped by his babysitter! Here it is! Here!"

I slap the phone on the table, but it's blinking out of power and goes black. Mom searches for her charger to plug it in and Dad swears again.

"Sean said his babysitter—"

"Paul?" he says. "Paul Landis?"

"His babysitter exposed himself and showed him pictures of boys with no clothes on. One boy. Then he made Sean be in some pictures." It was coming out stupidly. "He made movies of Sean and him. Him and his friend are taking movies at his house right now!"

"Owen—"

"Dad, just listen to me! The other guy took movies and Paul Landis said if Sean told anybody the pictures would go on the Internet but they were only for his friends now and only for a little while if Sean did what he said—"

I'm twisting myself up, but it's coming out now and I can't stop.

"Sean told me if I told anyone else they would go online, so I didn't tell anybody. It's been going on since June, since right after school ended, but Sean's bad now, really bad, and he's saying things about dying and you didn't see, nobody saw, nobody sees, and I couldn't tell,

190

but they're over there now and we have to stop them, here, look at the video. I was just there! Look!"

The stupid phone is up now, and they look and I look again. Then I run into the downstairs bathroom and throw up before I reach the toilet. I can't stop puking until everything comes out and there's always more to come out. Mom comes in with a spray bottle and a handful of paper towels.

"My God, Owen, I'm so sorry, so sorry." She's on her knees scooping up the puke and putting it straight into the toilet and flushing that and cleaning up more. I want to put my face into her chest and go dark and just stay there, but I'm shaking all over and gagging and puking until there isn't any more.

"I broke my promise, and everyone will know about Sean," I say, washing my mouth out in the sink. "I broke him."

"No, no," she says. "No, that's not true."

You know everything I know, so I don't need to say it anymore. I tell them and I tell them and I tell them, and even before I finish, long before I finish, Dad is on the phone to the police, saying Sean's address and the name, "Paul Landis. L-A-N-D . . . Right." Then my mom calls

Sean's mother in P-town and tells her in as few words as she can, trying to be calm, but her voice is cracking through all the words she has to say.

And that's it.

The thing is out of me now, the hate that choked me and kept me from talking is part of what I threw up, but the other huge thing starts, the thing that will take the rest of the summer and forever.

———————

Later that night, my dad comes into my room. He sits on the bed. I've been staring out the window. I've seen the police car crunching slowly up the driveway.

"Dad, I'm sorry I took your phone."

"Owen, no. Look. They've been at Sean's for hours, the police. He's been to the hospital and is home again. And now two officers are here. They want to ask you some questions."

"Did they catch him? The two . . . men?"

He shakes his head. "I don't think so. Not yet. That's why . . ."

I wipe my face. "I'll be right there." He gets up. "Dad. I'm sorry about before. I'm sorry I stole—"

He cuts me off with a strong hug. He holds me to him. "You did good, Owen."

My eyes sting, my throat tightens up. "I don't feel good."

"I know. But you did good."

Ginny pokes her head in the door while we're like that. "Mommy told me somebody hurt Sean."

My eyes flood up again. "Yeah."

"Will he be okay?"

"I . . . I'm sorry I yelled at you."

"Yes, honey, he'll be okay," my dad tells her. He doesn't know whether that's true or not. But that's what he says. Ginny gives me a flat, sad face and puts her soft little arms around me. Mom is on the landing outside my room now. I know she wants to hug me, too, but there are sounds downstairs. I hear the car idling in the driveway, the muffled crackle of a radio. Light is coming in the front door. The police are waiting for me.

I wipe my face. "Okay. I'm coming."

———————

While Mom stays upstairs with Ginny, Dad takes the chair next to me at the kitchen table. The interview with the police is a repeat of what I told him and my mom, except slower, with details. One officer stands with his back to the side door, the other writes it all down in a notebook, her walkie-talkie beeping and clicking. She tells us that Paul Landis and his friend, whose name is William Doyle, had already left Sean's house by the time the first police arrived. Even now the town is being searched, the Cape, the whole state.

Then she asks this: "Did he, Paul Landis, or his accomplice ever do anything when you were alone with them or when you were together with Sean Huff?"

"I never met the friend."

"All right, but I mean to you. *To* you? Did Paul Landis ever touch you?"

I shake. It's a normal question for the police to ask, but I shake. I look at my dad. His eyes are wet. He's searching my face. I glance into the officer's body camera and understand that I'm part of the story.

"No. No. Nothing like that. Never."

My dad shifts at the table, reaches his hand across to me.

That night I lie in bed. My bed. I think: Is it safe to be here? Sean's room is so much like mine, my room could be his. Am I safe?

———

I go over to Sean's with my parents and Ginny the next day. Ginny huddles close to Mom all the way down the sidewalk. By now it's past the middle of July, a bright, hot, hazy gold day. I'm sweating through my second shirt of the day by the time we stop in his driveway. Then, even before Mrs. Huff opens the front door, Sean plows past her and leaps off the porch stairs at me. His face is red, puffy, and he freaks out, jumps up and down and screams as my parents try to go to his mom, but she holds up her hand and they stop.

"Want! He . . . you . . . want . . . he . . . no!"

I back away across the lawn, farther and farther as he comes at me, and I try to understand what he's yelling. I finally do.

"He wanted *you*! He wanted me to get you over here so he could make you do it, too. More boys in his movies are better, he said. He was going to make you do it with me! I wouldn't. I said I would rather die. He was worse after that. I saved you. And you ratted on me. You showed everyone what a creepy ugly dead thing I am!"

I have nothing to say. I turn to ice. Sean saved me?

He shrieks all kinds of things and keeps going, screaming words that strike me like burning rocks or bullets or knives, until he tears back into the house and into his room.

Even from outside, I hear his door slamming with a crack, then things crashing as he throws stuff around his room and finally at the window. Glass shatters onto the lawn while he screams over and over until he goes dead silent and stares through the broken window at me. His eyes are blacker than anything. Mrs. Huff says nothing to any of us, just disappears inside the house and closes the door.

I stumble back to the sidewalk as Ginny clutches my mother's legs, sobbing.

My mom and dad try to tell me Shay is going through something they don't—and can't possibly—understand, and to give him time. "To heal," my mother says, but all that makes me think of is a wound, a huge, deep, bloody wound. I feel as if Sean's been blown up, and when his front door closed, it was like a door slamming shut in my life. I go to bed that night, not sleeping, my heart hammering for hours, unable to remember a time before Paul Landis destroyed our lives.

The next day, Mom calls his mother. "She wouldn't say much," she tells me later, "but she did tell me Sean hasn't spoken a word since we saw him yesterday."

I want to go silent too, and realize I nearly have. I look at her, wanting her to hold me, but she doesn't, just tells me more.

"When she finally knocked on the door of his room yesterday, Sean wasn't there. He must have gone out the window. There was blood on the broken glass. She called the police right away. While some of them searched for those criminals, others went out to look for Sean. We didn't know any of this. They found him hiding at the beach."

This surprises me, but I still can't find anything to say.

"I'm proud of you, Owen," she tells me finally. "Thank God you told us."

No matter what my mom and dad believe, telling actually doesn't help everything. Of course, the ugly story hits the TV news and the Cape newspapers. Paul Landis and William Doyle are named, but not Sean, who is called "an adolescent boy living on the Cape." It's sketchy at first, but it becomes clear when they talk about Paul's position at Old Sailors Church that the "boy" was a parishioner and lived in Brewster. It's starting exactly as Sean said it would if I told. Everyone will know. Everyone.

A few nights later we're eating dinner quietly, which is how all our dinners are now, and my dad gets a phone call. "Hello?" He listens, cups his hand over the receiver. "It's the police." He listens again. "Yes. Yes. Can I tell him?" Another few seconds. "Thank you." He hangs up.

"Tell me what?"

He's frowning, swallowing a couple of times, and Mom once again looks to take Ginny from the room, but Ginny says, "I know, 'Time to play.' It's okay," and she skips out, so Mom stays.

"Dad, what did they say?"

He takes a breath. "Some—some of the videos, like those creeps said, some of them are online. The police said they try to shut down sites, but there are loopholes and laws to get around, and those people are clever and it's hard to stop those kinds of pictures once they get out."

Mom shakes, her lips quivering, curses openly about "laws," then says we'll never lie again about anything ever. "We're going to tell one another everything and not keep secrets ever. Things are different now, no matter how we don't want them to be. We've been burned, too. We have to protect ourselves. By never lying."

We need it to be that way, she says, to keep strong as a family.

So that's a good thing.

The police and the lawyers are pretty quick to pounce on the case, but nothing shuts down. It only grows bigger. From the video I took, the police track the cameraman's car to Pennsylvania. He's not there, but I learn later from the newspaper that his wife—his wife!—rats on Paul so that she won't be charged, but she *is* charged because she knew about it, and she claims that Paul Landis is the one who set it all up, but the police say he wasn't, although they find he's done this in other towns with other boys. The story grows day by day, week by week, well beyond Brewster. Altogether over the next weeks, about a dozen people in different states are arrested. No one else from Old Sailors Church is involved. Just Paul Landis. Everyone there is shocked and sad and angry. But it still doesn't stop growing. Not long after, the newspapers mention that it was "a friend of the victim's video evidence" that broke the story.

In early August, another two police officers come with an agent from the FBI.

"We thought we were close to arresting William Doyle, the camera operator," the federal agent says, "but it turned out to be a false lead. At this point it's unfortunately too big to stop anything from going wide. It's already overseas. It may only take an instant, but once something's on the Internet, there's no controlling it. Your friend's nude images were saved thousands of times instantly, and we can stomp on a roach here and there, but they don't go away. That's the damn truth of it."

I can tell that Dad's ready to argue with him because he's so cold about it. But I nod and try to take it in like an adult would.

About the middle of August, they arrest Paul Landis in Florida and bring him back to Massachusetts. Because he pleads not guilty at what's called an arraignment, there is a preliminary hearing in late August. He's put in jail without bail until then. The judge says he'll try to escape, so he's just locked up. Good.

I have to appear as a witness in Orleans District Court, which covers things in Brewster. The preliminary hearing is not in a courtroom jammed with people and reporters and cameras, but in the judge's private chambers with attorneys. I find out that the cameraman is still "in the wind." That's how one lawyer puts it. "In the wind." Meaning, he's vanished. They can't find him. Which makes my skin crawl. One of the lawyers tries to say my video can't be used in court, but the other lawyers argue about that. The big trial will come later, but I hear from Mom that Adam Sisley from baseball said something, too. Once Adam saw the story in the Brewster paper he told his father, and Mom was in the newspaper office the day the reporter uncovered this from the police. What happened to Adam is nowhere near what Sean went through, but it's more testimony against Paul Landis.

"He just put his hand on my butt once, maybe twice, that's all," Adam tells me later. That was at our last game, two weekends before Labor Day, which is late this year. A couple of people on the team know what happened to Sean because Adam told them what he learned, and everyone pretty much put it together anyway, because nobody sees Sean around anymore.

Later that day, Kyle comes running across the field to me. "Good job, man," he says quietly. "You're something." He grabs my hand and pulls it to his chest and wraps his other arm around my back for a long minute. This is the first time I've ever done that kind of teenage hug. "You're Sean's real friend."

Each day I remember more of what Sean screamed at me when we drove to his house the day after I snitched on him.

"It's not your fault, Sean. None of it," I told him. "You didn't do anything—"

"No? Well, take a look on your computer to see what I *didn't do*. Everyone's going to know what I *didn't do*. They may not know me, but they'll know about that kid who does horrible stuff, the kid who takes off his clothes and his stupid pod. Owen, they were going to leave! Pack up and leave and it would be over. The pictures wouldn't go anywhere. Now? People are going to stare at my mom wherever she goes. They'll all know. How long before—does Ginny know what I do?"

I feel like just bones, standing in front of him. "You did it, but you don't do anything anymore. You didn't want to—it was a crime."

"It doesn't matter. Maybe I had to and maybe I didn't. I don't even know. But it doesn't matter. It's all going out there because of you, you jerk! Everybody's gonna know. *Everybody!*"

"No, they won't, because maybe it won't even go out there." I knew I was lying. He did, too.

"You're so dumb," which are not the words he really used. His voice was just hot, stale breath. I barely heard him, but I did. "I know those creeps. My pictures are going out and they'll never be gone. They'll always be there. When I'm old they'll be there. But that's fine, because I'm not even me anymore. I'm 'the boy who was raped.' There's no *me* anymore."

My blood turned to ice when he said that. He was careful not to say what I think he wanted to, that killing himself was still a thing he might do, but I remembered his words. I hoped someday they wouldn't be true, that Sean would be back, that we could hang together like before, but when he shouted those words his eyes were so dark, his face so twisted, I believed him.

"He had his pump on the day we went to see him," my dad said out of nowhere after that last baseball game. "The day after we called the police." Dad looked at me across the front seat of the pickup. "You could see it on his arm."

"His pod?" I said. "He always has it."

"Well, he could have deactivated it, couldn't he? Not put on a new one? Or he could use an insulin pen, right? Given himself a big dose? He can control it."

"Okay."

"I'm saying he cares. Even that day, right after finding out we told, as angry as he was, Sean cared about his health. It's a small thing, but maybe not so small. Maybe it means he cares a little about what happens to him. Sean's not going to do anything bad. Not necessarily. And he has good people all around him. His mother. She quit the shop, did you know that?"

"No."

"She did. She's with him all the time. Think about that."

Okay.

But I was still the only friend he told, and it would have ended, Paul assured him, but I went and told everyone and it grew into a huge thing that's still growing. You could say I had no choice. You could say that of course

Paul was lying about stopping the abuse. You could say I should have told someone first thing. You could say I was just pointing to myself and acting the hero by rescuing Sean.

Either way, he couldn't be my friend anymore because I told the world what he swore me not to.

A friend doesn't do that.

A friend keeps secrets for a friend.

Even the darkest ones.

Doesn't he?

The last weekend in August I see a FOR SALE sign on his front lawn. I see moving trucks come, but Sean and his mother have been gone for weeks. No good-bye. Just gone. I walk around the side of the house. The flower box under his window is just soil, no plants, the windowpane has been replaced. I peek inside. His room is empty, no furniture.

Over and over I hear the shattering of glass and see his face with eyes blacker than tar, and no matter what anyone believes, it's clear to me.

To Sean, I stopped being his friend at that moment.

At that moment, to Sean at least, I became the opposite.

TWENTY-THREE

A funny thing happens on the Cape in September.

The days are still warm, but as soon as the sun drops the air cools and turns blue like a deep blue flower. If you can believe it, the air is even clearer at the end of the summer than it is in June. Whites and blues and golds and greens burn with their own fire. Edward Hopper, the painter who lived on the Cape, caught that, too.

So. The evening before Labor Day I'm in my room, lying on my bed, staring at the green walls, trying to make my heart slow down. This is something I have to do every day, or whenever I think about Sean, which is the same thing.

It's going on seven, late for dinner, but everything else is so normal. My mom has just gone out for pizza. I hear Dad slowly setting the table on the patio. I look out and see Ginny near him, sweeping dirt and grass cuttings from the flagstones the way a five-year-old sweeps, mostly just rearranging the piles, when I hear shells crackle halfway up our driveway. Police? Mom? No. From the other window I recognize the minivan and run down the stairs.

I yank open the front door. "Sean!"

But like that afternoon weeks before on his porch, it's not him. It's his mother.

She's out of the car, brushing past the rosebushes, all green now and flowerless, and coming up to the step. "I can't really stay," she says.

Her hair is different, longer, a little wilder, no more angles. Her face is changed from the last time I saw her, too. Thinner. Calmer, maybe, but sad. She looks tired.

"You just missed my mom. Dad's in back—"

"I came to see you, Owen. Do you have a minute?"

I hear the clinking of silverware and the scraping of chair legs on the patio.

"Sure."

We sit on the front porch in the wicker chairs and just breathe for a couple of minutes before either of us says a word.

"How's Shay?" I ask.

She tries her best to smile, but it doesn't work. "Oh, Owen." That's all she says for a while. She's different than

I've ever seen her. She isn't scattered, fidgeting all over the place. She's *here.* Taking a deep breath, she starts.

"Sean's been horribly hurt. You know. It will t-take time." Her face breaks suddenly, and she shakes and sobs into her hands.

"I know. I'm sorry. I hurt him a lot."

"Oh!" she says. "Oh, Owen, no! Not you. You never hurt him. Never."

She fumbles in her bag for tissues. It's strange to see a grown-up shaking so much that she might fall to pieces. I'm shaking too, but that doesn't matter. She tries to calm down again by breathing slowly in and out.

"Can I come over to see him?" I ask. "I know you don't live here anymore, but sometime?"

She crumples a ragged tissue in her hands. "Sean doesn't want to see anyone right now. That'll change, I know it will." She looks across the wicker footstool between us. I think she's deciding to say or not say what she wants to. Maybe she's trying out different words for it. She doesn't speak for a long time, so I find myself saying it again.

"I'm really sorry."

She shakes her head from side to side, sniffling. "You were closer to him than anyone, Owen. If he didn't have you, he wouldn't have had anybody. You knew him better than I do. You're closer to him than I am right now."

"No."

"You are."

She leans far forward in her chair, her hair dangling over her face. She slides it back and says in a kind of whisper, "Sean wouldn't be alive except for you."

My throat gets thick. "That doesn't make any sense. I didn't—"

"You did," she says, softer now. "Do you know where we found him that night after you came over? The police and me and his father? You know, his father has been great, actually. He came right away. He's found us a place to live." A pause. "Do you know where we found Sean that night?"

My chest buzzes and my throat stings with acid. "At the beach, I thought."

"In a kayak he stole. He was paddling out into the bay. He was a half mile out before the Coast Guard could get to him. He wouldn't stop. They had to stop him."

"Where was he going?"

She covers her mouth with her hand. "You know where he was going and what he was going to do."

I shut my eyes and see waves, and tears seep out onto my cheeks.

"Thank God we got to him," she says. "We never would have found him. Or only later. But he didn't have a chance to do it then. And now I don't think he has those kinds of thoughts anymore. Not often, anyway. He talks to me a lot more than he ever did. He hasn't let me touch him, but he looked me in the eyes the other day. It sounds so small, but he hasn't done that for weeks. He's going to be Sean again because of you."

We don't say anything for a little while. She wipes her eyes. I try to calm the thunder in my chest.

"I waited too long," I say. "I stood there and waited and didn't do anything while horrible stuff happened."

"What about the rest of us?" Tears keep running down her cheeks. "Owen, what you did isn't the bad thing. It's the only good thing. It's the best thing you could do."

My parents tell me the same thing every day. Kyle too, whenever he sees me. They all keep telling me.

Mrs. Huff leans over her chair again and reaches for my hands. "I want to tell everyone to be you, Owen Todd. I want everyone to be like the friend that Sean has. Not every person has one. Not like you."

I'm too far from her when I cough out a sob, so she slides from her chair and kneels in front of me before I can get up. She hugs me for a long time, kneeling like that. It seems like an hour. I hear pattering from inside the house. Ginny's feet. I think she looks out, then runs back. A few seconds later the floorboards squeak. It's the weight of my dad coming to see. But he doesn't come out, either. The boards creak again and it's just the two of us.

The blue beyond her shoulder is turning purple. To-morrow will be bright, warm, one of the last days of real summer.

"Sean will hug me like this again, too," she says, pulling away and smiling at me through wet eyes. She seems so tired. Out of breath. I guess she would be, after every-thing that's happened. I sit there like a lump, shaking, my face wet and hot.

Her hand is on my arm, and it's hot, too. "He'll be all right because you love him and you told us. His thera-pist said that, and we have to believe it. You told us and ended it and Sean is still here. You did that."

I close my eyes and all the water flushes out and down my face. She holds my head and kisses the top of it lots of times. When I open my eyes, the late sun catches against the white trim on the opposite house, making a skeleton of its frame.

"Okay, then. You going to be all right, Owen?" She wipes her face with her tissue and smiles and stands up. "I think you are. I really should call you O, like he does. I have to go back home now. Well, it's not home yet. Sean is with his father and his therapist right now. His father moved nearby, did I say that? And his therapist, she's so good, so kind and patient. She says wonderful things about you, too. So now we have another person who gets to love Sean, because of you."

She looks at the time on her phone, which I remember she always used to do. "I have to leave pretty much right now. Sean asked me to come back soon. See? That's another good thing."

I wipe my cheeks. "You're not going to stay for the parade tomorrow?"

"Only if it's for you." She laughs, wiping her face. "No. I really have to go. It's a couple of hours' drive."

"Where do you live now?"

She keeps wiping her cheeks. "Sean doesn't want anyone to know, and I have to respect that. It's not Wellfleet, but that's where he keeps talking about. You went there a couple of times together, didn't you?"

Wellfleet.

"Once," I say.

"He told me all about the beach roses there. The white and the pink and how you like them. He does, too. We don't have any where we are now. Not nearby."

It's hard to believe that out of everything from that day on the beach—the waves, the sand, the girls in bikinis, the roses, and the wind—Sean remembers anything but the promise I made there and how I broke it.

"You'll tell me when I can come over?"

"I will." She smiles with her lips closed. "Soon, I hope."

And that's all of it. She gets in her minivan. It's the

same car she drove Sean and me home in on the last day of school. So much has happened since then.

Shay is hurt, he's beaten up, he's broken, but I want to think he isn't going to be that way forever, and everybody keeps telling me he isn't going to be that way forever because of me.

There's a short parade on Labor Day. It's a pretty dinky version of Memorial Day's two-hour float fest. It has a kind of sad, end-of-something feel to it. There are no pancakes, not that I would eat any, only a couple of vintage cars, a high school glee club float, a gang of bicyclers in costumes, and fewer veterans from the older wars. There are always fewer veterans, one parade to the next.

It's been a rough summer. Grandma. Sean. Things ending. Other things beginning.

By the end of the week, school will start. Ginny will enter first grade, and I find myself surprised for the hundredth time that we'll never be in the same school at the same time. But I get to see her every day at home, and I will for a long time, so I'm okay with it.

I'll go into sixth grade. For the first time in forever, my school won't have Sean in it. Maybe he'll be in another one somewhere else, if he's okay enough to go. Maybe he'll be in a place where he doesn't ever have to think about anything that happened here.

The trees in my yard and all over Brewster, the Cape, and everywhere are full and green and heavy with leaves, like they always are until the weather chills.

In the next few days, the vacationers will pack up their cars. Lined up like caravans, they'll drag themselves onto the highway. The town will be back to the rest of us, the roads will clear, the lines for go-karts and ice cream and pizza will thin down to half, then to a quarter, then to two or three people I'll probably know. I'm thinner, too, and a little taller. Over the summer I lost four pounds and grew two inches, like my mom predicted.

AUTHOR'S NOTE

I believe it was Philip Roth who, when asked to describe one of his novels, said, "It's about what it's about." I view *The Summer of Owen Todd* as a work of fiction not solely about any one thing. It's about the Cape, about baseball, karting, summer, boys, families. Still, at its core is a horrifying and often unreported crime: the victimization of a child, a boy in this story, by a trusted male adult. I don't believe that novels can or should properly accommodate messages, but readers can and do bestow on books the power to do more than tell a story. At best this book is only a whisper in the conversation about sexual assault, but a whisper is better than silence, and whispers can be loud, if enough of them join together.

I am grateful beyond words to Mary Jo, who was instrumental in the genesis of this book, and whose son, not as lucky as Sean Huff, didn't survive the trauma of his abuse. It was and is her passion that *not* keeping a secret about abuse is a heroic act. To Heather and Liam Staines, for their gracious and generous mom/son discussion of the daily details of type one diabetes. Any inaccuracies about this aspect of the story are, naturally, mine alone. To Erica Rand Silverman, who searched and searched until she found the perfect publishing house to bring this book out. To my editor, Joy Peskin, for accepting the story, and for her inspired and moving work in coaxing out and shaping its final form; I'm so happy to have a book at FSG again. To my daughters, Janie and Lucy, for being the loving people they are: you give me such hope. And as always to my wife, Dolores, for her unyielding support from the very beginning, when I decided to put a difficult story on paper. Her love for the characters is on these pages, too.

Victims and their families and friends who need information on how to deal with sexual assault or suspected abuse or who have any questions at all are urged to explore the resources of RAINN—Rape, Abuse & Incest National Network—at rainn.org. Their National Sexual Assault Hotline is free, confidential, and available every hour of every day. The number is (800) 656-HOPE.

Other organizations include the National Sexual Violence Resource Center (nsvrc.org); the various state-specific agencies associated with the National Alliance to End Sexual Violence (endsexualviolence.org); and the National Suicide Prevention Lifeline (suicidepreventionlifeline.org), which contains specific resources for young people and a chat line at (800) 273-8255. It should also be noted that in the aftermath of sexual violence victim advocates are available for both primary and secondary victims (like Sean's mother and Owen himself) to help at hospitals, court houses, and police departments. School counselors are trained to discuss a variety of difficult issues directly with students and can sometimes offer a young person the closest safe environment.

To use the terrorism catchphrase, if you see something, say something. Whatever you do, talk to someone. Children should always speak up, no matter how it might hurt to do so. If you suspect anything bad or uncomfortable is happening to you or a friend, tell an adult, a parent, a teacher, a person you trust. Better to tell someone than to remain silent. Better to lose a friend than lose a life.